The Secret
Treasures
of Oak Island

D0957895

The Secret Treasures of Oak Island

J. J. Pritchard

Formac Publishing Company Limited
Halifax, Nova Scotia
2002

Copyright © 2002 by J.J. Pritchard

All rights reserved. No part of this book may be reproduced or transmitted in any form or by any means, electronic or mechanical, including photocopying, or by any information storage or retrieval system, without permission in writing from the publisher.

National Library of Canada Cataloguing in Publication

Pritchard, J.J.
    The secret treasures of Oak Island /
J.J. Pritchard.

ISBN 0-88780-582-5
    1. Treasure-trove—Nova Scotia—Oak
Island—Juvenile fiction.
I. Title.

PS3616.R57S42 2002   j813'.6
C2002-903364-0

Formac Publishing Limited   First published in the
5502 Atlantic Street,   United States in 2003 by:
Halifax, N.S., Canada B3H 1G4   Orca Book Publishers
www.formac.ca   P.O. Box 468 Custer, WA
                                    USA 98240-0468

Printed in Canada

Table of Contents

To
Michael
&
Chrissie

1

Breath of Fire — 1608 AD

To touch them is to die," Shonuuk's father had warned countless times. And Matnaki's words were stone. Even a 10-year-old like Shonuuk could count the graves of his people.

When the first of the white men's great ships appeared, when Matnaki was a boy, the Mi'kmaq were as plentiful as the oak trees of the forest. They had been a thriving people like the neighbouring Abenaki or Cree. Now the graves outnumbered the living many times.

Today Shonuuk ignored his father's strict orders, as he had for the last few weeks. In his hiding place within the underbrush, Shonuuk could overhear the bearded men's twisted tongue. He smelled their foul bodies on the wind.

Sadness and death had been constant companions of the Mi'kmaq since the white man's arrival. The deaths were horrible. Death was no longer the peaceful passing of an elder, or the courageous end of a proud warrior. Death had become a mass of boils and sores covering the skin, raging fires burning from within, and endless vomiting with tortured bowels until one's very soul was spent. All these things ran through Shonuuk's mind as he crouched in the brush, watching the bearded men. Yet the scene fascinated him.

Shonuuk once had seen a great ship of the white men, who called his people *Tarrateen*. He had heard stories of the fur-gathering ships belonging to the men who called the Mi'kmaq *Souriquois*. But the men Shonuuk spied upon today had crossed the great water to this tiny island in ships unlike those.

Below Shonuuk's hillside perch were more white men than he could count. Numerous as the grey geese that flew overhead. Shonuuk had secretly watched them off and on for two weeks. Never had he seen men work so long and hard. They toiled endlessly, never seeming to tire. They began at first light and continued well into the darkness. They pushed themselves like slaves, yet seemed to work by choice. Their limitless stamina fueled Shonuuk's fascination.

"What could drive men so?" Shonuuk wondered. "Their chief must be great to breathe such spirit into them."

The white men's chief stood out from the other workers. He stood taller than Matnaki and was dressed in red clothing more brilliant than the setting sun paints the sky. The strange hat perched upon his head made him appear even taller. No one else was dressed in this manner. Shonuuk called him "Breath of Fire." Breath of Fire carried a large scroll, which he repeatedly unfurled, carefully studied and rolled back up before shouting orders to the multitude of men.

A much smaller man, carrying a large cloth hanging from a wooden pole, followed close behind Breath of Fire.

"It is curious," Shonuuk thought. "These men are as fearful of this large cloth as they are of Breath of Fire."

But Shonuuk was even more curious about what the white men were working on. They felled no trees with which to build a walled fortress or homes. These invading white men drove themselves day after day, night after night, digging an enormous hole in the earth.

Each year, Shonuuk and his family left the tribal lands for the solitude of this small island. Here the family would hunt, fish and gather acorns from the many oak trees. Shonuuk looked forward to this time of togetherness with his father, mother and sister. It was the time Matnaki taught Shonuuk the skills he would need for manhood. Shonuuk also liked exploring the island. But this year, the white invaders would cut Shonuuk's visit short.

The family made camp on the shore facing the setting sun so the grand island of their tribe was visible across the narrow channel. This year, Matnaki had forbidden Shonuuk from venturing to the island's eastern shore. But it was here, on the forbidden side of the island, that Shonuuk first saw the great ships of these strange white men, and where he now spied upon their labours.

The white men had dug trenches that converged at a small hole close to the shore. The trenches, shallow at the beach where they began, gradually became deeper.

"How clever," Shonuuk observed. "At high tide, the sea water will run down the channels. But why would the white men want to bring salt water inland?"

There were many puzzles about these men.

No sooner were the deep ditches dug, than Breath of Fire's men threw in large stones, small boulders and a curious brown fur that the bearded ones brought from their ships. The trenches were then refilled and carefully hidden.

"It is as if the ditches never existed," Shonuuk thought.

Further inland was a second hole — a pit beyond anything Shonuuk could have imagined. It grew deeper and deeper day after day. Relentlessly, tirelessly, they took out bucketful after bucketful of dirt. While the mouth of the shaft was no wider than a long canoe, three nearby mountains of dirt spoke to the hole's unnatural depth.

"Surely," thought Shonuuk, "this hole is as deep as the great water."

But this morning the digging stopped. Carefully concealed in his hiding place, even Shonuuk could sense something important was happening.

Out in the bay, one of the ships launched a small boat. Breath of Fire stood at the front of the boat, leaning on several huge wooden chests as men paddled toward shore. Upon landing, the bearded men swarmed about the chests, carefully lifting them onto a long litter. Ten men, five to a side, hoisted the litter's stout poles to their shoulders. The large boxes loomed above their heads as they proceeded slowly towards the hole.

Breath of Fire walked in front of the weight bearers with the small man carrying the large cloth close behind. The chests were carried to the edge of the deep pit and placed onto a small log platform. Shonuuk saw the platform, with a long rope affixed to each corner, lower the workers into mother earth as a hundred or so white men clustered around the edges of the precipice.

Shonuuk held his breath. He had never spied on the white men from such a close distance. If one should look up to the small hillside, they surely would see him. Cold sweat ran down Shonuuk's sides.

Breath of Fire unlocked one of the thick wooden boxes and raised the lid slowly. Shonuuk could clearly see inside the chest. His eyes widened in disbelief. Then Shonuuk slipped! To his horror, his foot dislodged a large rock that noisily tumbled down the hillside.

The foreign savages began shouting and yelling in their strange tongue, and many pointed up the hillside directly at Shonuuk. They saw him! Many of them drew swords. Others raised deadly *thunder-sticks*. Six of the bearded men began running up the hill where Shonuuk crouched, frozen in terror.

"Run!" Shonuuk screamed within himself.

Shonuuk burst from the brush and raced up the hill. Choking back tears of terror, and gasping for breath, he ran for his life.

"To touch them is to die," echoed through Shonuuk's head with each pounding beat of his heart. He could hear the white men shouting close behind. He could hear them crashing through the underbrush through which Shonuuk swiftly darted. Racing along a deer trail, Shonuuk ran faster and faster, his small heart pounding harder and harder.

"To touch them is to die. To touch them is to die." Shonuuk ran wildly until he, too, was blindly plunging through the underbrush where no trail existed. Finally, when he thought his insides would burst, Shonuuk collapsed, unable to take another step. His chest heaved in pain. As he fought to catch his breath, he listened. He could no longer hear the white men yelling and shouting. He could no longer hear them clumsily floundering through the forest. Save for his own gasping lungs, all around him was quiet.

"Today I have outrun death," Shonuuk thought breathlessly. He vowed upon his ancestors' spirits that he would never return to spy again.

Shonuuk waited until midday to venture from the safety of where he lay. Silently and cautiously he made his way toward the centre of the island to the huge rocks and boulders Matnaki had shown him weeks earlier. This particular grouping of boulders leaned against and atop one another. Over time, smaller rocks, soil and plants had taken hold above the three massive stones, creating a solid roof on top of the rocks. Nature had created a secret chamber, or cave, which only Shonuuk and his father knew existed. Here, Shonuuk's 10-year-old imagination created fierce battles between himself and the warriors of many tribes.

The entrance to Shonuuk's hidden sanctuary slanted peculiarly to one side, following the lines of the rocks that formed it. Ivy crept down the face of the rock, partially hiding the cave's entrance. After squeezing through the narrow crevice, Shonuuk paused to let his eyes adjust to the dim light.

Shonuuk turned to face a smooth stone wall in the small chamber. Over the past weeks, unbeknownst to his family,

Shonuuk had painstakingly drawn the white men's project in surprising detail with the charcoal tip of a partially burnt stick. He had even crushed berries with which to paint Breath of Fire's brilliant coat. The picture was nearly complete.

Shonuuk crouched down and sketched the two large chests he had seen this morning. He scraped the charcoal tip on the ground into a finer point then slowly drew the contents of the wooden box he had so clearly seen. Near the likeness of Breath of Fire, Shonuuk drew the small man with the large cloth on a pole. Shonuuk stepped back to admire his work. That's when a man's shadow fell across the cave wall.

Shonuuk fearfully spun around to see his father, Matnaki, standing at the cave's narrow entrance, clutching a large water-filled gourd in his left hand.

"Shonuuk, you have been gone all morning," Matnaki said. "It is time to return to camp. We have fresh deer to dress."

Shonuuk rushed to block Matnaki's path, hoping his father would walk no farther into the cave.

"I will come with you now," Shonuuk said obediently.

Matnaki looked down and saw the scratches covering his son's face and arms from his panicked flight through the woods. Matnaki reached out to Shonuuk's chin and raised his son's face to the light.

"How could my son be so clumsy in the forest?" Matnaki questioned. "Did you frighten a mother and her cub, or..." Matnaki's voice trailed off. He saw the picture on the wall behind Shonuuk.

"What is this?" Matnaki demanded. "Is this what chased you through the woods? Answer me, Shonuuk!"

"I only meant to watch them," Shonuuk said, unable to meet his father's angry glare.

The veins stood rigid on Matnaki's temples and neck. He shook with rage — furious that Shonuuk had openly disobeyed him, and terrified that his only son had come into contact with the infectious white men.

"Did you touch them, Shonuuk?" Matnaki shouted. "Did you touch them?"

"No!" Shonuuk said, meeting his father's eyes.

"After all the sorrow our tribe has endured at the hand of the whites. After all this, you disobey my word!" Matnaki shouted. "You have endangered our family and our tribe with your carelessness!"

"I meant no harm," Shonuuk said.

"And you honour their likeness in this way," Matnaki said pointing to the detailed drawings.

"I meant no..." Shonuuk tried to answer.

"Enough!" Matnaki bellowed.

In a fit of rage, Matnaki hurled the water-filled gourd at the picture. It smashed against the wall and the spring water splashed over much of the drawing.

"No!" Shonuuk shouted, rushing toward the mural. Matnaki caught him by the shoulders and shoved him aside.

"Until this day I have never been ashamed of you," Matnaki said, his anger souring to bitter disappointment. "But today you shame me. We will leave the island tomorrow. I will decide your punishment tonight."

Matnaki angrily walked past Shonuuk and exited the small cave.

Shonuuk stood alone in the cave, tears burning his dark eyes. He looked at the cave wall.

"He didn't have to do that," Shonuuk thought. Defiantly, he picked up the charcoal-tipped stick and carefully drew a large "X" in the middle of the cloth he had drawn, completing the figure.

"Come now!" Matnaki's voice boomed from outside the cave.

Shonuuk threw the charcoal stick to the ground and wiped his tears. He stormed out of the cave, never to return. As he dutifully returned to camp at his father's side, Shonuuk had no way of knowing that he would be the last person to enter the hidden chamber for nearly four hundred years.

2

Summer Vacation

PEOPLE are stupid."

That's what my dad used to say.

"People will believe anything or follow anyone who has an easy smile and a gift for gab. Just like sheep."

Maybe that's why my dad was afraid of believing in anything. But I don't think people are stupid. I just think people need to have hope, or someone who gives them hope.

* * *

Only two weeks into summer vacation and I was already bored. The weather had been unusually wet for late June. I didn't like TV or computer games. I was tired of reading, and my little brother was really beginning to annoy me. My best friends were at camp. They'd invited me to go, but I wasn't ready to be gawked at by a whole new bunch of kids — not yet anyway.

It had been a difficult school year. I'd missed two months because of the car accident, and when I returned, everyone acted differently. I knew they meant well. They were all sympathetic and tried not to stare, but I just wanted things to be the way they were. I wanted to look the way I used to look.

For quite a while, a day didn't go by, an hour didn't pass, during which I didn't wonder why this had happened to me. What had I done to deserve this? There must have been an easier way to teach a 14-year-old that life's not fair. But after a few months I came to believe there *was* some reason. That's what kept me going, kept me positive — most of the time. It was the idea that everything happens for a purpose, and I just didn't know mine yet. I clung pretty hard to that belief. It kept me afloat in very dark waters.

My name is Emma Day Morgan. I was named after my great-great-grandmother, but everyone calls me Em. I live with my family in Brackendale, a small town about 65 kilometres north of Vancouver, British Columbia.

I guess nowadays we're an unusual family; a throwback to the 1950s. Mom and Dad were raised right here in town. They dated in high school and got married when my dad graduated from Simon Fraser University. They had two kids, a boy and girl, of course, and we've lived in the same small house ever since I can remember. We're a very white-bread family.

My dad, John, is only 39, but he looks and acts 10 years older. My brother, Joel, and I sometimes wonder if he wasn't born middle-aged. His hair isn't grey yet, but he's become bald, and he combs his hair over from one side to cover it up. Dad's the one who shows up at the family picnic wearing shorts with black shoes and white socks. He just doesn't get it.

Dad's been an accountant for Griffin Markets, a grocery store chain in Vancouver, for 14 years. I know he's not happy. He never invites Joel or me to see where he works, like other dads, and he never talks about work around us. I remember him saying it didn't make sense to work your way up in a company since you'd just become a target for layoffs. Better to stay where you were.

"If you stick your neck out, it'll only get chopped off," he'd say.

Alice, my mom, is the same age as Dad. She's very conservative except she wears goofy glasses with bright blue frames. She says she's had them for 20 years and I believe it. She didn't even take them off for their wedding pictures.

A lot of people underestimate my mom because she's so small, only five feet, and so patient. But mom's surprisingly strong in quiet ways. She insists we say grace before dinner, she works the hardest to keep the four of us pulling together in hard times, and she never complains about getting up at 4:30 a.m. to work in Brackendale's 24-hour copier shop. Mom understands Dad better than anyone, but she never gives him advice. I think she feels people have to figure out their problems for themselves.

* * *

It was Saturday, 8:30 a.m. Mom and Dad had just finished breakfast and were reading the morning paper. The dirty dishes were still on the table.

"John," Mom said, looking up from the paper. "Did you

see this? Jake's going to be in Lions Bay tomorrow night to make some sort of speech."

"Yeah, I saw it," Dad said without looking up.

"Well, weren't you going to tell anyone about it?" she asked. "The kids would love to see him."

"He left me a voice mail a couple days ago about it," Dad said, still reading his paper.

"Well?"

He put the paper down and looked across the table.

"Allie, he's in town promoting another one of his get-rich-quick schemes. I've seen and heard enough of them. I don't need to hear another one," he said. "It's embarrassing!"

"John, he *is* your brother," she said. "The kids wouldn't forgive you if they found out Jake was in town and you didn't tell them."

"Uncle Jake's in town?" Joel asked excitedly, walking into the kitchen.

"Yes," Dad answered with a grunt.

"Cool!" Joel said. "Em, Uncle Jake's going to visit!"

Joel is 11 and he's not so bad as little brothers go, but he can certainly be a jerk when he sets his mind to it. Joel, always popular, is very outgoing and good at sports. In fact, that's how he lost one of his upper eye-teeth, playing football in the street. You can see the gap when he smiles.

The most revealing thing about Joel happened when he was only nine. It had snowed a week earlier. Most of the snow had melted, except under the trees and where the sun couldn't reach it. Joel and I were tagging along with some of the older neighbourhood kids who had the brilliant idea of throwing snowballs at cars. Don't ask me why we agreed to do such a dumb thing. Anyway, since the snow had partially melted and refrozen, the snowballs were more like iceballs.

We were on the edge of the woods and planned to pelt the cars as they drove around a blind corner. As the cars went by, the rest of us lost our nerve, so we talked Joel into doing it. Like I said, he was only nine. We heard a car coming and just before it appeared, Joel threw a rock-hard snowball that smashed loudly onto the windshield with a loud crack! Just as Joel released the iceball, we noticed the white car had blue lights on top — a police car! The car screeched to a halt. We tore off into the woods — except Joel. He stood his ground and took his medicine. I still tease him about sitting in the patrol car while the chief constable spoke with Dad, but I secretly admired that Joel hadn't run away like the rest of us.

Joel and I don't get to see Uncle Jake often. When we do, he entertains us for hours with amazing stories of travels and adventures in places we barely knew existed. We know he exaggerates, but it's still fun to listen.

I got off the sofa and rushed into the kitchen.

"Uncle Jake's going to visit?" I asked eagerly.

"He's going to be in Lions Bay," Dad said. "But I don't know if he'll have time to come up here."

"Oh, of course he'll have time," Mom added. "He always makes time to visit."

"What's he in Lions Bay for?" I asked.

"Another treasure hunt?" Joel questioned.

"It's just a short speech," Dad explained, downplaying it as much as possible, "probably to raise money."

"Listen," Mom said, referring back to the newspaper, "Brackendale's own 'Indiana Jones,' Jake Morgan, will speak at Westside Community Centre at 5 p.m., Sunday. Mr. Morgan, 37, a graduate of Brackendale secondary school, has travelled throughout the world in search of treasure from numerous ancient civilizations. Most recently, Morgan spent seven months in Brazil searching for the mythical lost city of Quixtempa. However, the expedition was unsuccessful."

"That's an understatement," Dad interrupted.

"John!" Mom said. She continued to read. "Morgan will answer questions and present a slide show about the technology-based equipment that will be used in his expedition to solve the famous Money Pit mystery."

"The Money Pit!" Joel interrupted. "I've heard of that! No one knows who dug it or what's buried in it!"

"The Money Pit is a deep pit on Oak Island, a tiny dot of land off Nova Scotia," Mom continued. "Morgan believes the pit contains a significant quantity of gold, contraband buried centuries ago by pirates, who were known to frequent the area in the late 1600s and early 1700s."

Mom glanced at the other side of the page. "There's another article here about the history of the island."

"Real pirate treasure!" Joel said. "Let me read it."

"Can we go?" I asked. "We're not doing anything tomorrow night."

"Hold on, both of you," Mom said. She looked back to the article.

"Tickets are eight dollars per person and five dollars for students and seniors. All proceeds will go to the Lions Bay Library's Historical Society."

"Well, can we go?" Joel pleaded.

Mom set down the paper and looked at Dad.

"Well?" she asked.

Dad let out a long sigh. "I suppose so," he said reluctantly.

3

The Money Pit

ATTENTION! May I please have your attention? If you will take your seats we can get started."

The nervous man at the front of the hall seemed to be swallowed up by the large podium he stood behind. All Joel and I could see of him were his horn-rimmed glasses and the top of his bald head. It was obvious from his shaky voice that he didn't enjoy standing in front of the 400 people seated in the community centre.

"My name is Peter Millard. On behalf of the library's Historical Society, I'd like to welcome all of you to tonight's presentation," he read from his notes in a trembling voice, never so much as glancing up at the audience.

A handful of stragglers stopped whispering and made their way to their seats as the doors to the hall closed. Although there were still a few empty seats, this was a remarkable turnout for a Sunday night in Lions Bay.

My family sat in the second row. Joel squirmed in his seat. I thought it was exciting that so many people had come to hear our uncle. Dad, on the other hand, was not excited. He wore a sour frown with his arms crossed sternly across his chest. He was not the least bit impressed that his younger brother was the centre of so much attention.

"This evening we have the pleasure of hearing from our own Jake Morgan, who grew up in Brackendale and attended SFU," Millard droned into the microphone.

"For all of one semester," Dad whispered loudly to Mom.

"Mr. Morgan's current project involves an attempt to salvage the legendary Money Pit in Nova Scotia," Millard continued. "The pit contains a buried treasure that has frustrated treasure hunters for more than 200 years. Tonight, Mr. Morgan will provide an in-depth analysis comparing modern salvage techniques to the crude methods of the past."

Millard finally looked out at the audience, greatly relieved that his portion of the program was coming to an end.

"It is my pleasure to introduce Jake Morgan!"

Uncle Jake is 37, two years younger than Dad. His black, curly hair makes his green eyes appear unnaturally brilliant. You had to look hard for the Morgan family resemblance, but it was there in the shape of his nose and mouth. Yet while Dad and Jake had similarities, Dad's features had grown soft, and Uncle Jake's were hard. They were the same height, but Jake always seemed taller.

When Joel and I were little, we wondered why we didn't have any cousins. Uncle Jake had been married briefly, but had told us, "It just didn't take."

The best thing about Jake was his laugh. It wasn't a timid chuckle, but a throw-back-your-head, laugh-at-the-world kind of laugh that filled the room. Not everybody appreciated that kind of manner.

One Thanksgiving, Dad and Jake got into an argument about something. Dad called him a flake who wasted his time and other people's money chasing rainbows. Uncle Jake just threw back his head and laughed that big laugh. He said, "John, you're probably right, but they'll never erect a statue to a bean-counter, and they don't write songs about someone who sits behind a desk!"

But mostly, Uncle Jake had an energy about him. His philosophy of life was something like you'd read on an inspirational calendar — "Reach beyond your grasp," "Life is not a dress rehearsal," or "Make bold plans." Uncle Jake was the kind of person whose belief was so strong in whatever he talked about, it just made you want to believe right along with him. His enthusiasm was contagious.

Jake strode confidently to the front of the auditorium and firmly shook Millard's hand. He clipped a small portable microphone onto his lapel and greeted the audience.

"Thank you," he said. "I'd like to thank the Historical Society for arranging this presentation on such short notice. The society requested that I limit my remarks to a discussion of modern-day salvage methodologies. Based on my personal experience, that would include comprehensive computer data analysis, computer-enhanced ultrasound imagery and ultraviolet satellite photography."

There was a collective groan from the group.

"That's not why I paid my eight dollars!" one woman called out.

"Come on, Jake!" another man shouted. "Tell us about the treasure!"

Even I had to admit the topic sounded boring. If Jake dimmed the lights for his slides, half the people would fall asleep.

Jake tried to continue, but the audience wouldn't quiet down.

"What about Oak Island?" a man asked. "That's what I want to hear about!"

"Save the fancy stuff, Jake. Tell us what you're up to!" someone else shouted.

Many in the audience had grown up with Jake. They knew what they could expect. They hadn't come to hear about high-tech computer gizmos in modern salvage work. They wanted a story.

Jake stepped out from behind the podium and abandoned his assigned topic, to the delighted applause of the audience. As the applause faded, he deliberately paced across the front of the hall, rubbing his chin, staring intently at the floor, seemingly lost in thought. Everyone anxiously leaned forward. Those in the rear craned their necks. For nearly two full minutes, Uncle Jake walked back and forth, oblivious to the hundreds of onlookers. His silence was unsettling. People began to fidget and whisper.

"Is something wrong?" a woman asked her neighbour.

"He's forgotten what to say," another quietly said.

Everyone believed Uncle Jake was getting himself ready to speak, but really, he was getting the audience ready to listen. Then, just when the tension was nearly unbearable,

Uncle Jake turned to the audience and began.

"Who among you has not dreamed of treasure; of secret, gold-filled chambers hidden for centuries from civilization, or of ancient chests overflowing with golden goblets and coins? How many of you have held real gold — not a bracelet or ring, but a bar of pure, solid gold? Who cannot marvel at its beauty? Who would not be entranced by gold's glimmering brilliance? And who among you have felt its power? It is that same power, the same seductive allure that has compelled all mankind since time began — pharaohs and kings, peasants and thieves, wise men and fools. For that is what we seek — to unlock the riddle of Oak Island, and wrestle forth from the earth a golden treasure unlike anything the world has seen.

"Yet strangely, the Oak Island treasure carries a curse. For 200 years it has defied the cautious and killed the careless. It is the last great mystery in the western hemisphere. Many say it cannot be solved."

Jake paced as he spoke. It was as if it required all his strength to contain the storm that raged inside him. Within a few minutes, his shirt was stained with perspiration and thin lines of sweat trickled down his temples.

"The story begins in 1795 when a young man was exploring Oak Island. In a forest clearing not far from shore, he discovered a mysterious depression in the land, as if a large hole had been dug and refilled. There were whispered tales of pirates sailing in those waters a hundred years earlier and legends of a lost treasure. He returned the next morning with two friends and, equipped with picks and shovels, they began to search for whatever was hidden.

"Half a metre down they uncovered a layer of strangely arranged flagstones; a type of stone not found on the island. Excited by their discovery and sure they were close to treasure, they quickened their pace. At a depth of 3 metres, they found a platform of partially rotten oak logs, firmly embedded in the sides of the pit. Now there was no doubt — something was down there! But after more hard hours of furious digging, at 6 metres they encountered yet another layer of decayed oak logs. It took all their effort to remove them and return to their digging. As darkness approached, they reached the 9-metre level and found yet another oak platform. Unable to remove these logs, and with no light left, they ceased their frantic digging and abandoned the island. But the memory of the treasure pit haunted them for years."

Uncle Jake's voice rose and fell like a great wave, crashing around us one moment, then receding to a gentle whisper, as if the thunderous voice had never been there at all. The audience was spellbound.

"Nine years later, in 1804, the three returned to the island with a crew. This time, they hoped, they would recover their prize.

"They dug past the 9-metre level, to 12 metres, and discovered another oak platform. Deeper and deeper they dug. At 15 metres, another platform, and at 18 metres, and at 21, and at 24. Every 3 metres they found a platform of oak planks. That was all they found until they reached the 27-metre level.

"It was here that they uncovered what was considered the

most important clue of all — a large, flat stone inscribed with a strange cipher or code."

Jake paused and lowered his voice to a mere whisper. Every person strained to hear. The hall became deathly quiet.

"Upon translation it read, 'Twelve metres below two million pounds are buried.' However, since that time, no one has been able to locate the inscribed stone to verify the treasure hunters' claim. It seems to have vanished.

"The flat stone rested on another oak platform, like the eight before it. The oak beams were removed, and the work continued. They were now so deep they required lanterns to light the depths unless the sun was directly overhead. Beneath the 27-metre level something else occurred. The soil, previously dry, became waterlogged. For every two buckets of earth they hauled out, they removed one of water.

"Then, at 30 metres, they struck what they thought was another wooden platform. But it turned out to be far more than that. As they removed the first plank, one worker claims to have heard a strange suction noise. However, it being dusk, they decided to stop for the night.

"In the morning, the workers returned to find the pit filled with water! They bailed until their hands bled, but were unable to lower the water level. Discouraged and defeated, they gave up and left the island for good. But word spread of the stone's inscription, and the legend of the money pit grew.

"The island was left deserted for half a century, until

1849 when another attempt was made to solve the mystery. This group used a horse-powered mining drill to bring core samples to the surface. Once again they drilled down to 30 metres when the drill struck something. It was another platform, but it was followed by 30 centimetres of space, then 10 centimetres of oak, then one-and-a-half metres of loose metal pieces, and 10 more centimetres of oak. The drill then pierced a final platform of spruce and struck hard bluish clay.

"A diary kept by one of the workers claims the auger drill contained pieces of gold coins. Yet once again, that evidence has disappeared. It is widely believed the auger drilled through a large oak chest, its top and bottom 10 centimetres thick, filled with coins.

"The group dug another shaft next to the original pit, hoping to reach the chest from the side, avoiding the flooding that had plagued the first expedition 45 years earlier. But like before, the water seeped in and filled the pit to sea level."

Jake walked among the audience as he wove his mysterious tale, stopping frequently to emphasize a point and looking directly into their eyes with a piercing gaze. But Jake wasn't preaching. It was as if he was sharing a special secret that bound him with every person. The audience was captivated by every word, each gesture, and every artfully phrased sentence.

"In 1861, a third expedition journeyed to the island with a remarkable bailing system involving 63 men and 33 horses. They worked in shifts around the clock, but despite all their efforts, they were unable to reduce the water level below 27 metres. There seemed no answer to the mystery — how did the water find its way into the pit?

"One afternoon, a worker saw something on the beach that made his blood run cold. Water was gurgling *out* of the beach and running down toward the low tide! He tasted it. It was salt water! That afternoon, the entire crew of 63 men began digging up the beach. Their discovery made it clear that this was no ordinary treasure.

"The Money Pit was booby-trapped! The pit's design included an ingenious flood system. Two underground tunnels, approximately 125 metres long, connected the deepest levels of the Money Pit to a reservoir near the shore. The tunnels, designed to fill with sea water, were filled with large stones and covered with coconut fibres. The fibres acted as a crude filter system against silt and debris. The Money Pit had been built so that sea water could flow in and out of the secret drainage system.

"Here was the answer! Once treasure hunters reached a certain depth, sea water rushed in, flooding the pit. It was an insidious but brilliant feat of engineering.

"They tried unsuccessfully to block the channels. They tried dynamiting the channels, but that, too, failed. Finally they gave up, but not before two workers were scalded to death in a boiler explosion. And so began the talk of a curse.

"In 1897, another group fell under the pit's seductive power. This time, steam-driven pumps lowered the water level down to 29 metres and more core samples were drilled to pinpoint the location of the treasure. At 38 metres, the drill encountered the same oak chest, but the drill was unable to capture any of the loose metal pieces inside. However, when the drill was removed and cleaned, another puzzle was added to the mystery. Stuck to the auger drill was a small piece of sheepskin parchment containing the letters *vi*. There is no way to know what this parchment was from — a document, a bible, a manuscript, perhaps a map; no one knows. And like the expeditions that had come before, this one, too, ended in failure.

"There were three or four other attempts during the 1900s, but each time the efforts failed due to cave-ins, flooding and deaths."

Jake glanced at the clock on the back wall of the Community Hall. He'd spoken much longer than he'd intended.

"Some believe the ghosts of those who dug the pit stand guard over it, reaching out from the grave to foil all efforts to raise the treasure. Perhaps that's why all the evidence and artifacts mysteriously disappear. Some believe the pit is cursed, and the floodwaters will run red with the blood of any man who defies it.

"But I do not believe that. I believe 38 metres down lies an enormous oak chest, filled with a hoard of ancient coins, each individual coin worthy of a museum, their total value beyond calculation. And I believe we will be the ones to seize it. Thank you!"

It took several moments for the enthralled audience to realize the presentation was over and to thank Uncle Jake with thunderous applause.

4

The Agreement

WE waited 20 minutes for Jake to finish answering questions. A lot of people wanted to know more about the Money Pit, others just wanted to say hello, and a few asked if they could still invest in the project. We approached as he finished with the last person.

Dad and Jake quickly shook hands. Uncle Jake gave Mom a big hug and then put his arms around me and Joel.

"That was great!" Joel said excitedly. "Do you think you can find the treasure?"

"We're sure going to try," he answered confidently.

"I hope you don't have dinner plans," Mom said. "We'd love to have you over."

"Are you sure that wouldn't be any trouble?" he asked.

"No trouble at all. I bought steak and fresh corn," Mom said.

"Great!" Jake smiled. "Then I accept!"

"You can tell us about the Money Pit," Joel said.

"I'll be happy to, and I've got something I'd like to discuss with your folks as well," he said looking to Dad and Mom.

"What about?" Dad asked suspiciously.

"Relax, John. I've got an idea I think you'll like," Jake said.

"We can talk at home," Mom added. "Do you need a ride?"

"No, thanks," Jake replied. "I've got a rental. I'll meet you there."

I walked into the parking lot with Uncle Jake while the others retrieved their coats. It was good to be out in the cool evening air. The hall had become hot and stuffy. The parking lot was jammed with people scurrying to their cars.

"Well, Emma," Jake said. "Tell me — how are you getting on? Have you gotten back to your daily routines?"

"Most of them," I said. "Some routines have been harder than others."

"I can imagine. You've been very brave these last few months," he said.

"I guess so," I said. I was uncomfortable with the whole bravery label. It just meant I disguised my fear well. As much as I loved Uncle Jake's attention, I didn't want to talk about me. My kind of bravery was forced upon me and, frankly, I resented it. Uncle Jake's bravery was of his choosing, and much more impressive as far as I was concerned. I wanted so badly to be his kind of brave. I hoped something would rub off on me by spending time with Uncle Jake, so I'd be able to rise to the occasion like him — with good cheer, enthusiasm and self-confidence. "What do you want to talk to Mom and Dad about? Oak Island?"

"I think you could definitely say that," he answered with

a mischievous grin. "But I better wait and talk to them first."

"You sure didn't get a chance to talk about technology tonight," I said. "All anyone wanted to hear about was the treasure!"

"Em, my girl, you're absolutely right!" he smiled.

"Look at all these folks," Uncle Jake gestured toward the parking lot. "They're as different as night and day. But they all came for the same reason. They're searching for inspiration. Like poor souls lost in the desert burning up with thirst. It's something they've got to have.

"Every day these folks go about their ordinary lives, work in their tedious jobs, and come home to the same old houses and apartments. It's the same thing, day after day after day. But people want something bigger, Em, something brighter. They want a beacon, shining in the distant night, that can lead them out of their ordinary little lives and into something grand!"

"And that's you?" I asked.

Jake laughed.

"No, Em, it's not me. It's treasure — this treasure! It's solving a riddle some say can't be solved; a mystery centuries old. It captures their imaginations and makes their hearts beat faster! It takes all these people back to their childhood when a pirate's chest of gold was just waiting under the very next shovelful of dirt in their own backyards."

Jake paused and looked thoughtfully across the parking lot.

"But mostly it inspires people, Em. And for a brief moment, things don't seem quite so ordinary."

As we waited for the family to catch up, I realized the Oak Island treasure was also my Uncle's dream.

After dinner, Dad sent Joel and me away so he could talk with Uncle Jake. Joel and I stretched out on the floor of his bedroom with our ears pressed against the heating vent. We could hear everything that was being said in the living room.

"Well, what is it this time, Jake?" Dad asked sarcastically. "Out of money? Need a loan to tide you over? Or the name of a good lawyer to fend off another court case?"

"John!" Mom scolded.

"It's okay, Alice," Jake replied. "I don't expect you to understand this business, John. I'd be the first to admit treasure salvage is a screwy line of work. I'm not here to ask you for money. You've always made yourself perfectly clear on that score."

"When I think of how Mom and Dad lost most of their savings by believing in you..."

"Grandma and Grandpa?" Joel whispered. "Did you know that?"

"No," I whispered back. I hated this kind of trouble between my two favourite men. I wished my dad and Uncle Jake could be friends.

"We've been over that a thousand times, John. I can't change what's happened," Jake said. "I repaid them as best I could. Why is that the only thing you can talk about lately? That was 10 years ago!"

"You just don't get it, do you?" Dad said angrily.

Dad wasn't always so bitter and mean-spirited. My earliest memories were of his hands encircling mine, making everything safe. A while ago I looked through an old photo album to see if he had changed a lot. It seemed to be a different person smiling back at me from those faded pictures. I think he blamed himself for what happened, even though it wasn't his fault. He was driving the car when we were hit. I remember waking up one night in the hospital. He was quietly sitting next to my bed in the dark with tears streaming down his face. It was the only time I'd ever seen my father cry.

"Jake," Mom broke in. "What did you want to talk to us about?"

"Well," Jake said, "I know you haven't got any plans for the kids this summer, and Lord knows you two could use a break. I know it's been a stressful time for everyone. Why not let Emma and Joel come with me to Oak Island?"

I couldn't believe my ears! I looked at Joel with my mouth and eyes wide open.

"What?" Dad exclaimed.

"John, it'll be great for them!" Jake said. "A month of fresh air, exercise, plus it's beautiful over there this time of year."

"All the way to Nova Scotia?" Dad said.

"They'll learn some history, explore the island and see how a salvage operation really works," Jake explained. "And if we do find treasure, it'll be an adventure they'll remember the rest of their lives!"

Joel and I couldn't stand it any longer. We were up and running to the living room in an instant!

"Is it dangerous?" Mom asked.

"Of course not," Jake assured her. "These things run like a business. They're actually a bit on the boring side. We've also got one of the best crews I've ever assembled."

We burst into the living room.

"Can we go?" I asked excitedly. "Please!"

"Please, please, please, please," Joel pleaded.

"For a month — camping out?" Dad said. "Em's not ready for that, Jake."

"Yes I am," I said, even though I didn't believe it completely. But here was an escape from the boredom. "It wouldn't be any problem at all."

"I can help her," Joel said dutifully. That would be a first, I thought with a laugh.

"John," Mom said, "she's spent so much time cooped-up inside this year. It would be good for her — in a lot of ways."

"They could fly with me in few days," Jake explained.

Dad looked around the room. He could tell by our faces that we all thought it was a fabulous idea and that Joel and I were dying to go. He looked at Uncle Jake.

"You promise they won't go into the shaft, or even anywhere near it?" he demanded.

"Of course," Jake answered quickly. "You've got my word on it." He extended his right hand out towards Dad. Dad just stared at him without moving a muscle.

"On your word as a *Morgan*?" Dad asked.

Dad and Jake looked each other in the eye for what seemed like the longest time. The slow ticking of the clock on the mantel was the only sound in the room.

Finally, Jake replied, "On my word as a Morgan."

Dad reached out and they shook hands, this time like they meant it. It was odd, but it seemed like something passed between them in that moment.

"Yes!" Joel shouted, jumping around the room.

"Excellent!" I added excitedly. We were going to Oak Island! It was beginning to look like this summer would be salvaged after all.

5

Oak Island

UNCLE Jake was unusually quiet during the six-hour flight from Vancouver to Halifax, Nova Scotia. Joel spent most of the time reading comic books while I read a few magazines and watched the in-flight movie, which wasn't very good.

I think a lot of people become introspective on airplanes because of those "what if" moments, like when you hit really bad turbulence. The passengers' collective gasp is followed by intense silence as everyone nervously clings to their armrests. Or that instant right after takeoff when the pilot eases off the throttle, you feel the plane hesitate, and in that split second you wonder if that was supposed to happen.

I was looking out at the clouds and paused to study my reflection in the plane's window. I had been avoiding mirrors as much as possible lately. My auburn hair was cut off to my shoulders. I'd inherited pensive dark green eyes from my dad's side of the family. My nose was just slightly turned up and, thankfully, the freckles that splashed across my cheeks were beginning to fade. Sixteen months of wearing a retainer had straightened the picket-fence teeth I had in grade school. The face staring back at me was the same one everyone said was so cute — I just wondered if that really mattered anymore.

Thirty minutes before landing, Jake brought up the subject of the Money Pit. I think he could finally lower his guard and share his honest concerns about the expedition now that he was away from the publicity and the audiences.

"Before we get to the island I want you both to understand there's a chance we may not find anything," Jake said. "Salvage work is a lot harder than most people think. If it was easy, someone would have retrieved this particular treasure a long, long time ago. No one has because of all the problems involved."

"Like the flooding?" I asked, anxious to learn everything I could about this mysterious island.

"That's the most obvious challenge," he stated. "Another is the sheer lack of evidence from earlier efforts. We have a few of the journal and diary pages that some of the expedition workers kept, but a lot of the legends are just that — legends."

"What about the flat stone with the secret code?" Joel asked.

"The one that said, '*Twelve metres below two million pounds are buried*'?"

"Yes," Joel said. "Isn't that proof?"

"If it existed," Jake said. "But it doesn't. It mysteriously disappeared within weeks after its discovery. Most historians believe it was a hoax, dreamed up by the treasure hunters to create excitement about the pit and raise money. Besides, think about it, why would anyone hide a clue 27 metres underground? It makes for a good story, but it's not proof. The fact is, there is virtually no physical evidence that there's a treasure buried down there — just the few surviving scribbles from the first expedition; which we hope are accurate."

"But you believe there's treasure, don't you?" I asked, wanting to believe it myself.

Jake looked away thoughtfully for a moment before looking me in the eye.

"Yes, I do," he said with conviction.

"Well, if anybody can get it, you can," Joel said loyally.

"I hope so, Joel," Jake said gazing back out my window. "I hope so."

Upon landing at Halifax International Airport, Jake rented a car for the 90-minute trip to Chester, which would be our nearest town. The tourist brochure said it was founded in the 1700s as a small fishing village. It really was a beautiful little town, particularly by the wharf where boats were moored. There were some small shops and restaurants along the waterfront. To get to Oak Island we drove down the coast about 10 kilometres to the causeway that was our link to the mainland.

"Take a look," Jake said, pointing ahead.

"That's Oak Island. It's shaped like a figure eight," he explained, "and about eight kilometres around. The Money Pit is on the island's eastern side, half a kilometre from shore. You can see the centre of the island is still pretty heavily wooded, mostly evergreens."

"No oak trees?" I asked, scanning the island for its

namesake.

"Supposedly, when it was first settled in the 1700s, it was covered with oak trees. But today there's only a single oak tree alive on the island."

That seemed kind of eerie.

"The island's highest point is 15 metres above sea level," Jake said. "There's some big rocks and boulders up there, and if you stand on the highest rock you get a great view of the Atlantic Ocean out to the southwest."

Jake was warmly greeted at the island's small boat landing by a large man in dirty work clothes.

"Welcome back, boss," the man said, enthusiastically pumping Jake's hand.

"How're we doing?" Jake asked.

"Ahead of schedule," the man said proudly. "I'll brief you later."

"Kids," Jake motioned us closer. "I'd like you to meet Doug Richfield. Doug's our crew foreman and head of operations. Doug, this is Emma and Joel. You've heard me talk about them. My favourite niece and nephew."

Doug Richfield looked like he belonged in one of Joel's comic books. He stood nearly two metres tall, had a boot-camp haircut and was greying at the temples, a ridiculously large handlebar moustache, and the massive arms of a professional wrestler. Doug oversaw the crew, the equipment, the supplies, the logistics — he really ran all the day-to-day aspects of the expedition. He never went anywhere without his clipboard, a two-way radio clipped to his shoulder, and a Palm Pilot in which he meticulously maintained the expedition's work schedule. But most importantly, Doug was Uncle Jake's closest friend. He had been on all Jake's expeditions. I came to realize that Jake valued Doug's advice and ideas above anyone else's.

Doug greeted us warmly and I felt an immediate affection for this trusted hulk.

Jake led us to the edge of the excavation area within the enormous work site, which encompassed the area of two football fields. A yellow Broderson crane towered above us. Jake climbed into the crane's white, fibreglass bucket, and instructed Joel and me to do likewise. It came up to our chests and was a bit of a tight squeeze for the three of us.

"Best way I know to see the area," Jake smiled. "Take her up, Doug."

"Sure thing," Doug replied, climbing into the cab and starting the crane's huge engine. "Ready on your signal."

"Let's go!" Jake shouted above the engine's roar.

The crane gradually reeled in the cable until the bucket began to rise. We reached about 6 metres above the ground. Just as the bucket stopped swaying, and I thought I could relax my grip, the boom arm began to extend skyward until we came to a stop 12 metres above the work area.

It was scary at first, being so high up and tightly squeezed into the observation bucket. But once I began to relax, it was great. A refreshing breeze cooled my face and neck, and the ever-so-slight swaying was relaxing, like an old-fashioned rocking chair. Like Jake had said, it provided an excellent view of the campsite and work area.

One end of the work area was a miniature city of 30 or

more red nylon tents — each unmistakably labelled "Recreation Equipment." Nearby, a double-wide aluminum trailer acted as the expedition's portable laboratory and headquarters. It held the more sensitive equipment, as well as some explosives and the artifacts found thus far on the project.

The rest of the clearing was filled with an array of construction and excavation equipment — mud-covered backhoes, coils upon coils of cable, brightly coloured nylon rope, and boxes of supplies. Three diesel-powered generators supplied electricity as the diesel engines constantly sputtered. Dredge pumps, hoses of all sizes, and stadium-style lights attached to long aluminum poles ensured that the work could continue around the clock. There must have been 40 or 50 workers beneath us.

The site of the infamous Money Pit was small by comparison. The arm of a small crane hung over the gaping hole in the earth, approximately 6 metres in diameter. An orange plastic construction fence ringed the pit. Three-metre-high, interlocking aluminum support pipes were stacked nearby.

At the far corner of the work site, a great deal of equipment was roped off and hidden under large blue tarps. I could just make out stacks of 200-litre metal drums not completely covered by the plastic.

"What's under the tarps?" I asked. I hoped my questions wouldn't bother Uncle Jake, but they didn't seem to, so far.

"That's off limits," Jake said seriously. "For the time being, that's my little secret."

"Off limits just for us?" Joel asked.

"For everyone," he answered.

"And you won't even give us a hint?" I persisted.

"Nope," Jake grinned. "It's probably the most important element of the expedition. That equipment is going to solve the flooding problem."

"What is it?" Joel asked.

"All in good time, Joel," Jake replied.

Once the observation bucket safely touched down, Jake introduced us to the second key member of the expedition — Marion Johansen.

Marion seemed an unlikely candidate for Uncle Jake's inner circle. Only in her early 20s, she was a tall, wiry long-distance runner who wore old-fashioned horn-rimmed glasses. Marion was the expedition's historical expert. Doug later told us that Marion's area of expertise was actually Egyptian history. Apparently, Marion's father was a friend of Jake's who thought it would be a good idea for his daughter to work on the expedition during the summer to escape the university archives where she was working. Jake said she had done a good job of getting up to speed on the history of the island and the surrounding area.

Just before nightfall, Joel and I called Mom and Dad on a satellite phone to tell them we'd arrived safely. Mom said she was glad to hear the enthusiasm in my voice. It would be the first time of many in the weeks ahead.

6

Digging for Treasure

I didn't sleep well that first night. Joel and I each had our own small tent, pitched in the middle of camp, with a cot for our sleeping bags. It wasn't the excitement of being part of a real treasure hunt, or even the new surroundings that kept me awake. Twice during the night I was awakened by the sound of a coyote or dog howling far in the distance. It didn't sound frightening or sinister, but like the call of a lonely animal in the darkness. Both times I sat up, listening intently in the dark, only to hear the wind outside.

In the morning, Joel and I ate an unusually late breakfast. We were still getting used to the four-hour time difference and I could see we'd have to adjust to the food as well. I quietly confided to Joel about the howling. He hadn't heard anything, but he had his own mystery.

"Check this out," he said, handing me a tightly folded piece of paper. "It was under my pillow this morning, Em. I know it wasn't there last night."

I carefully unfolded a brittle, yellowed piece of newsprint. Scrawled in pencil, in a child-like hand, were the words: "I'll help if I can." It gave me the creeps.

"What does it mean?" I asked.

"How should I know?" Joel replied. "Do you think we should show it to Uncle Jake? I don't want to look like a cry baby."

"Let's tell him," I suggested. "It might mean something."

Every morning Jake assembled the entire salvage team of 46, mostly men, for a daily meeting he called Project Update. Jake, Doug and Marion outlined the objectives for the day and explained anything unusual that had been discovered. Normally the meetings convened before breakfast at 6:30 a.m., but Jake had delayed today's gathering so Joel and I could attend.

As we reached the half-circle of workers gathered around a wooden table, we showed Jake the note.

"Was anything stolen from your tent?" he asked.

"No," Joel answered. "I don't think so."

"Well, it looks like someone's having some fun at your expense," Jake said. "We've got a couple of jokers in the crew. But I don't like the idea of them going into your tent at night. I'll mention it at the meeting. Nothing to worry about."

Jake stepped into the centre of the workers gathered around the table. He stood on one of the chairs so that he could be seen.

"Good to see you all again," he said. "We'll make this brief so that you can all get back to work. Doug, why don't you go first?"

"Fine," Doug said. "Yesterday we reached the 16-metre level. The fifth support length is now in place, so we have protection to 15 metres. We had a few problems, but over-all, the aluminum piping is working like a charm."

"What problems?" Jake asked pointedly.

"Nothing major," Doug said. "When we were lowering the fifth piece through the fourth, it jammed. Took us an hour to straighten it, but we're okay now."

"Good," Jake replied.

Jake and Doug had stumbled upon an ingenious solution to the normally slow and tedious process of digging into the earth and then reinforcing the shaft's walls against cave-ins. They had acquired what amounted to a set of huge tele-scoping aluminum pipes, 12 in all, left over from a govern-ment project in the Arctic. Each of the pipe structures was just over three metres tall. Each length was progressively smaller in diameter. The first section was five metres in diameter; the last only two metres across.

They reminded me of wooden Russian nesting dolls. When you open one, you find a smaller one inside, and then a smaller one inside that, and so on. It made digging into the pit faster and safer than ever before.

Once the first section of pipe-like structure was dug in three metres below the surface, the second was carefully lowered down inside the first. Then as the work crew dug down the next three metres, the support piece was gradually lowered, providing complete protection against cave-ins without having to stop to build wooden support walls. When the second support pipe was fully extended down to six metres, the first and second pieces were sealed with eight pressure clamps, and then the third support piece was lowered into the pit.

Jake explained that if we'd been able to see the finished underground structure, it would look like a huge telescope, 38 metres long, five metres in diameter at the top, narrowing to two metres at the bottom.

Before lowering each support section into the pit, Doug attached 10 wireless flow sensors to the outside of the curved aluminum sides. These measured pressure and water. The flow sensors would give advance warning if the pit was in danger of flooding.

"What's the condition of the dirt we're removing?" Jake asked.

"Pretty damp," Doug answered.

"How about the flood tunnels?"

"We've found one," Doug said, "We're having trouble locating the second. If we have to, we can go down another three metres just relying on the pumps."

"How many of you are working on locating the remaining tunnel?" Jake asked the crew. Five workers raised their hands.

"Doug, that has to be our top priority. The success of the entire expedition rests on finding both flood tunnels! How many of the crew can we put on it?"

"I can move seven more onto that team," Doug said. "Any more than that and we'll lose progress on the hole itself."

"Any safety issues while I was gone?" Jake asked.

"Nothing serious," Doug explained. "Stinson dislocated his shoulder, but he'll be back on the job tomorrow."

"All right, thanks," Jake said. "Marion, any new discoveries of historical interest?"

She stepped forward to address the crew.

"While you were gone, we found a number of things," Marion explained, pushing her glasses higher on her nose with her pointer finger. "First, we found a half-dozen hand tools that look to be from the 1965 expedition. We've started to pull up old support timbers that look like they were from the late 1800s. Two days ago we found a leather horse bridle."

"That must be from the 1861 group," Jake surmised.

"That's what we've assumed, as well," Marion agreed.

On the plane to Nova Scotia, Jake had explained that one of the biggest challenges was to separate the artifacts from the time the treasure was buried, and items left behind from salvage attempts. The first treasure hunters were on Oak Island in 1795, so their relics might be museum pieces in their own right.

"Anything else?" Jake asked.

"Stacy found two crude iron nails at the 14-metre level," Marion said. "We had to dig a bit sideways from the main shaft and that's where she found them. They're pretty corroded, and there are no markings, but they're definitely pre-1800."

"Good work!" Jake said to a short, black-haired woman. "Doug, can we get down to 18 metres today and lock in the next support piece?"

"And locate the second tunnel?" he asked.

"Can you do it?" Jake asked.

Doug looked at his crew thoughtfully.

"Give us until dusk and we can," he finally answered.

"Just two more things for the benefit of the group," Jake said to everyone. "First, I'm not opposed to practical jokes, I like them myself. But let's stay out of each other's personal belongings and use good judgment. Fooling around causes distractions, and up here, distractions can mean injuries, or fatalities. Let's stay focused!"

Jake had said that for Joel's and my benefit. However, looking at the crew's hard and determined faces, I had trouble believing any of them would do something as silly as slipping a note under Joel's pillow.

"You've all done a great job so far," Jake said to the group. "You've made exceptional progress since last week. We've set a demanding schedule and you're two days ahead of it. You can all be proud of yourselves. But you've all heard my promotional speech, so I won't go through that again."

Most of the crew smiled, being all too familiar with Jake's canned speech.

"But I want to underscore something — to *all* of you," he said looking at Doug and Marion. "Together we have the means to solve the greatest mystery in treasure hunting. This crew is second to none. Each one of you has been hand-picked as an expert in your field. We have the finest equipment and technology available for a rapid, pinpoint excavation. What took past salvage groups months and months, we'll be able to accomplish in a few weeks.

"Most importantly, for the first time in 200 years, we

have a real solution to the flood tunnels that have defeated every previous expedition."

This was the second time I'd heard Jake refer to solving the puzzle of the pit's flooding. When Joel and I asked him about it, all he'd say was "wait and see."

"We're on the verge of accomplishing something that will put each one of us into the history books," Jake continued, "and in the process, put quite a few dollars into our pockets. In return, I ask for your continued commitment. It'll mean two more weeks of a grueling work schedule, little sleep and putting up with Ed's cooking."

That brought laughter to most of the group. I was glad to know it wasn't just me being picky.

"But if we stick together, this will be the experience of a lifetime — and something you'll be proud to tell your grandchildren!"

After the meeting, Joel and I walked back toward the portable lab with Jake, kicking at stones and glad to be on such a great adventure. I could handle bad food, and getting dirty, just to enjoy this feeling of freedom.

"I've got a surprise for you," Jake told us. "They should be behind the portable. Come have a look."

We walked around the side of the small structure. Leaning against the aluminum wall were two gleaming new mountain bikes. Both were fully loaded — 21 gears, front and back shock absorbers, racing grips, an air pump and water bottle, a small storage bag in front, knobby tires, even a headlight. Mine was a brilliant emerald green, my favourite colour. Joel's was a flaming red. They were awesome!

"Are they ours — to keep?" Joel asked excitedly. "I mean, even after we go home?"

I have to admit I was hoping for a positive answer.

"Absolutely!" Jake grinned. "I've missed so many of your birthdays, these are probably long overdue. I asked your mom about the colours. I hope they're okay."

"They're fantastic!" I beamed, in disbelief. "Thanks, Jake!"

They really were fantastic. Joel and I were riding bikes at home that we'd both outgrown. These were far beyond anything we could have got on our own to replace them. I was sure I could handle it.

"Thanks a million," Joel added.

"I put a few things in the front bag," Jake said. "Extra tire tubes, a patch kit, flashlight, even a few high-energy bars. The island's criss-crossed with over-grown roads and old trails. I thought this would be a good way for you to get around and explore the island."

While we adjusted the seats, Doug approached Jake. He looked serious. He pulled Jake aside. Joel and I kept our heads down, but our ears were taking it all in.

"Jake, we've got a serious problem!" Doug said quietly.

"What?"

"We just got an e-mail from the Nicholson Group," Doug said. "They're backing out! They didn't say why, but they've put a stop-payment on their cheque. They won't even talk to us. They've referred us to their lawyer."

"We had an agreement!" Jake exclaimed. "They signed a contract!"

"I know, but they seem to think they can change their minds."

"Okay, I'll call them," Jake said, sounding tired.

"Jake, that was the money for the second half of the expedition," Doug said in a loud whisper. "Without it, we don't have anything left. Nothing! Not even enough for food, let alone to pay the crew."

"There's nothing left?" Jake said with concern.

"You said get the best of everything," Doug explained, "I did. I was counting on the Nicholson money."

"All right." Jake turned his attention back to us. "Why don't you two take some time to explore the island? I've got a situation here to attend to. Be sure to use those helmets; some of the terrain is pretty rough."

Joel and I were too excited about our new bikes, and the opportunity to explore on our own, to give much thought about Uncle Jake's situation. We never dreamed it might derail the entire expedition.

7

Riddle of the Cave

WE rode our new mountain bikes out of camp and up a steep, narrow dirt road. More a weed-choked trail than a roadway, it was the only road on the island. Joel and I didn't know exactly where we were going. The road seemed to be heading toward the centre of the island. This was the first time I had been on a bike since the accident. I hadn't been sure I could even ride a bike anymore. That's because I have a prosthetic arm from the car crash. On this new bike everything seemed possible. If I had been on my old bike, I would have had to stop and walk up the steepest parts of the road. But the additional gears on this bike made riding uphill a lot easier. As we crested the hill, we passed a grey, weather-worn shack, long ago deserted.

I found a small clearing in which to take a short break. One side of the clearing was encircled by evergreens, and the other side bordered a vine- and blackberry-tangled jumble of boulder-size rocks, probably dropped by a glacier a million years ago.

"This bike is great!" Joel said enthusiastically. "We should find some jumps."

"I'll pass," I said, laying the bicycle down gently then plopping down cross-legged next to it.

"You can take pictures of me *getting air*," Joel said.

"Joel, you never *get air*," I said, leaning back against a tall hemlock tree. And why did he think I had a camera? "The most you ever get off the ground is a small bump!"

"It is not," he argued. "What about the jump I made in the driveway? I must get half a metre in the air when I go over that!"

"A couple of *centimetres*," I corrected him. I knew I corrected him too often, but I viewed it as my job as the big sister.

On the far side of the clearing, a fat grey squirrel with a small pine cone clamped firmly in its mouth, scampered across the ground. It momentarily paused, nervously looked in our direction, and then skittered behind two trees growing against two of the huge rocks. Joel silently began stalking it.

"Leave it alone," I said.

"Shhhh," Joel replied quietly.

Joel crept to where the bushy tail had disappeared.

"He's gone," Joel said, disappointed.

"What a surprise," I said sarcastically, happy for the squirrel's escape.

"It's got a nice little stash of pine cones over here," Joel said. "Come look."

Squirrels are notorious for stripping fir and pine trees of green cones during the summer and hiding them for a winter stockpile of food. I'd read about hikers finding huge stockpiles containing thousands of pine cones. Joel had found about 100 cones amongst the huckleberry bushes growing against one of the huge rocks.

Joel cautiously reached down and pulled away some of the bushes to reveal a hole in the rock side.

"There's a rabbit hole or something," he called to me.

But as he pulled away more and more underbrush, the hole became bigger, until Joel realized what he'd discovered.

"Em, it's a cave!" Joel called. "Get my flashlight from the bike. Get both of them!"

After I retrieved the lights, Joel shined his inside. There wasn't much to see. The floor sloped up steeply into darkness. It looked like an animal's den.

"Let's go inside," he suggested.

"No way! There's probably a bear inside," I replied.

"I'll go a little ways in and tell you what I see," Joel said.

The two trees grew right next to the boulders. Joel slithered around them to squeeze in through the opening. He shined his light around the interior while his feet still stuck outside.

"Come on, Em," he urged. "It's a little bit dirty, but it's cool. There's sort of a ramp to crawl up, but then it opens up into a little room."

"I'm not sure I can get through there," I said, looking at how I'd have to contort myself to get around the trees.

"I'll help you," he answered.

It took me a lot longer than Joel to wriggle through the narrow gap between the trees and rocky hillside. Joel had been all the way inside for several minutes by the time I crawled up the sloping entry. The air inside smelled dry and dusty. The small chamber was about three metres long, two metres across, and two metres high. The grey stone walls were smooth and covered with a thick layer of dirt and grime. The ground was a spongy layering of dry, decomposed leaves.

I directed my light towards Joel.

"I'm glad you went through first," I told him. "You're covered with filthy cobwebs. You look like a ghost. It's disgusting!"

"Big deal," he said wiping them off. He held the flashlight under his chin to make a frightening face.

"EMMA!" he said in a pathetic attempt to be ghoulish.

"Stop fooling around," I told him. "Is there anything in here?"

"Nothing," Joel said. We shined our lights around the ceiling. Joel was right — there was nothing inside.

"It would make a cool fort," he said. He pulled my *Tru-Fit* ball from his pocket and tossed it against the wall of the cave, catching it as it bounced back to him.

"Your ball doesn't bounce very well," he said. He threw the ball and caught it again.

"That's not what it's for," I said. "Stop doing that! You want this place to cave in?"

"It's solid rock, Em," he said, throwing the ball particularly hard. He missed it on the return and it bounced wildly around the small interior, coming to rest by my feet. As I reached down to retrieve it, my shoulder rubbed against the wall, coating my shirt with dirt.

"Look at my shirt," I complained to Joel. In a way it was his fault. "It's filthy. Help me brush this stuff off."

Joel stared dumbly at me with wide eyes.

"Joel, the least you can do is help me. Joel. JOEL!" I finally shouted.

He slowly raised his hand, pointing to the wall directly behind me. I turned and jumped back with a jolt. Staring back at us, from where I had brushed against the wall, was the crude drawing of a man's face.

* * *

It took Jake, Marion and one other member of the crew all day to remove the thick dirt from the chamber wall, as well as a foot of decomposed material from the floor.

Uncle Jake worked all night, and in the morning he returned to wake Joel and me so we could see the extent of our discovery. It wasn't the cramped working space that made the removal process so slow. Marion insisted the work proceed like an archeological dig. Alternating between delicate excavation brushes and minute blasts of compressed air, they cleared centuries of grime from the wall's surface taking care not to damage the drawing hidden beneath. The small floor area was plotted and mapped with grid lines. Each spade full of debris was painstakingly sifted and examined for artifacts. I didn't mind missing that part of the expedition. Besides, they didn't find much — lots of decayed leaves, a few small animal skeletons, a large amount of dried animal dung, and a mostly decomposed stick.

The two trees in front of the cave were cut level with the ground so the crew could get in and out. Jake said they counted the rings, and the largest tree was 203 years old.

The cave, its floor completely cleared, seemed slightly bigger. Even Jake could stand up in the cave without having to hunch over. A high-intensity, battery-powered lantern flooded the cave wall, highlighting even the smallest detail of the drawing. Marion was trying to photograph as much of the drawing as possible.

Marion made her way over as we entered and exchanged a high-five with Jake.

"Major find, Jake! Major find!" Marion said excitedly. "You know how rare native cave paintings are in this part of the continent? Come on over kids and have a look."

The drawing was remarkable. Although it never reached a height of more than one metre, it stretched the full three metres of the chamber's length. The charcoal mural featured many men holding sticks or tools surrounding a large, black circle. Three small hills stood nearby.

One particular portion commanded our attention. Near the black circle stood several men, one of whom was holding what must have been a large flag. And next to him was a box-like shape — a treasure chest!

Joel and I understood Jake's excitement. This was a picture of the treasure being buried here on Oak Island. Centuries ago, someone had witnessed the excavation of the pit and had reproduced the remarkable scene on the wall of the cave.

"Does this solve the mystery?" I asked, proud of having been part of the drawing's discovery.

"I don't know how much Jake already told you, but this probably creates more questions than it answers," Marion said, adjusting her glasses. "But it does document that something was buried here a long, long time ago."

"How old is it?" I asked. "Is there any way to date it?"

"We'll send bottom-most samples to be carbon dated," she explained. "The lowest level — the oldest — can give us a general idea about when the drawing may have been done."

"How long will that take?" Joel asked.

"We have to send it to Toronto," Marion replied. "The soonest we can get results is about three weeks."

"We'll be done by then!" Joel blurted out.

"Unfortunately, it's the best we can do on short notice," Jake said.

"You know, Jake, there are a couple of things about this that don't add up," Marion said, fiddling with her glasses. "Normally, cave paintings were done by the tribal chief or holy man."

"Okay," Jake nodded, listening intently.

"Yet most of this drawing is really low to the cave floor, indicating an unusually short man, who wouldn't have been made chief. Secondly, drawings like this recorded rituals or were a way of honouring something. But the tribes in this area detested the Europeans. You wouldn't draw your enemies like this. It doesn't make sense."

Jake good-naturedly slapped Marion on the shoulder.

"You're too negative, Marion! Let me tell the kids what we agreed it does reveal."

Jake squatted closer to the drawings.

"We figure all the men here were workers. They're all holding tools or shovels," Jake said, pointing to the far right-hand side of the wall. "The black circle in the middle probably represents the pit itself. This other hole by the water must be the flood reservoir. The three little hills are probably mounds of dirt. There would have been lots of that."

"And this must be the treasure ..." Joel said, reaching out to touch the box-like shape on the wall.

"Don't touch that!" Marion screamed. She nearly leapt out of her shoes as she seized Joel's hand. All three of us jumped at her panicked outburst.

"I'm sorry," Marion said. "It's the oil from your skin. We don't want anything to affect the drawing. It's a museum-quality artifact!"

"You know, he *is* the one who found it, Marion," Jake said calmly.

"I know, I'm sorry. I've been working too long on this," Marion said wearily.

"Anyway, Joel, you're right," Jake said. "We believe that's the treasure. And here's the maddening part — you can see something was drawn inside the square, something in detail."

"The smudged part?" I said.

"Yes," Marion replied. "Near as we can tell, the large smudge, or smearing, is water damage."

"At some point, centuries ago, the cave must have

leaked," Jake explained. "Water must have run down the wall, blurring this large area of the drawing."

"It may have happened fairly soon after it was drawn," Marion theorized. "Amazingly, it doesn't appear to have ever happened again."

"Look over here kids," Jake urged, pointing to a spot in the centre of the water damage. "See how the red colouring is blurred in with these figures?"

"Yeah," Joel answered.

"We think that was intentional colouring; that the holy man or tribal elder who made the drawing coloured one or more of the figures."

"But there is one clue that wasn't ruined by the water," Jake said. "Look closely at the flag."

Joel and I leaned closer. In the centre of the crude flag was a large "X."

"X marks the spot," I said. I was joking but Marion looked at me like I was serious. She sure didn't have a sense of humour about any of this.

"Jake, the X on the flag, combined with the red colouring sounds very British," Marion said. "Eighteenth-century British soldiers wore red, and the X could be the Union Jack flag. They were certainly in the area during the 1700s."

"I thought of that too, Marion," Jake said, rubbing his chin. "I've been thinking about that most of the night. It sounds reasonable except for one thing."

"Uncle Jake," Joel said, trying to interrupt.

"Hold on, Joel," Jake said, squatting even closer to the flag. "Look at the attempt at detail on all the images. It's crude, but whoever did this had an astonishing eye for detail. The flag only has an X on it — nothing else. If it were the British flag, it would have lots of criss-cross lines. And wouldn't the lines also be red? Why were only one or two figures coloured?"

"Jake!" Joel said again.

"Shhh!" I scolded Joel. "Stop interrupting!"

"Come on, Jake," Marion said, exasperated. "You can't try to understand what some tribal priest did two or three hundred years ago. We'll never know that."

"What I'm saying is, based on the rest of the wall, that's probably exactly what the flag looked like!" Jake said firmly.

"If it's not British, what else could it be?" Marion asked.

"What about pirates?" Joel finally said.

"Pirates?" Marion said with surprise.

"That's exactly what I was thinking," Jake said. "Go ahead, Joel."

"Well, everybody thinks pirate flags always had the skull and crossbones on them. But most of them didn't. Most of them had crossed cutlasses, like swords, on them," Joel said breathlessly. "I read a book about it."

"Crossed cutlasses that make the shape of an X," Jake said, thoughtfully looking at Marion.

"And its nickname wasn't the Jolly Roger. It was *Le Jolie Rouge*, which was French for the beautiful red," Joel finished.

Would wonders never cease? Every now and then my little brother would say or do something to make me proud. This was one of those times.

"What about the red clothing?" Marion asked skeptically.

"Couldn't one of them have worn red?" Joel asked.

"Who? Captain Hook?" Marion asked sarcastically. "Jake, the pirate theory has too many flaws. The pit's design is an engineering marvel. Not only that, it required a large, organized, disciplined and obedient work force. Now does that sound like pirates to you?"

"I don't know," Jake admitted.

"We'll know for sure in a few weeks," I said encouragingly. "Won't we?"

Jake was quiet for a moment, then brightened. I detected that mischievous spark in his eyes. He sniffed the air.

"Can you smell it?" he asked. Joel, Marion and I looked blankly at each other.

"I can smell it!" Jake said dramatically. "Treasure! I can smell chests of gold doubloons, pearl necklaces, and crowns encrusted with diamonds, emeralds, rubies and sapphires!"

Good old Uncle Jake! His kidding around helped break the tension. When I thought about it, it was also why we were here — chasing the dream of buried treasure.

"Oh, I can smell it all right! I can smell a pirate skeleton clutching a cutlass with one hand, and gold coins in the other!" he said, gesturing wildly. "Come on, Emma, you can smell that can't you?"

"Yes, I think so," I played along.

"Me, too!" Joel said.

Jake laughed hard at himself for a moment, and then just as quickly grew serious. He put a hand on Marion's shoulder.

"We're getting closer, Marion. We really are!"

"I know," she agreed.

"I'm going to call in the press," Jake said, deciding on the spur of the moment. "This dispels any doubt that there's something down there. The investors will like the publicity, and the public should know that we're getting close to something really big."

But it would take several more weeks before we'd fully understand the secrets hidden in that cave drawing.

8

Goop

NOW, two days behind Jake's original schedule, the second and final underground floodway was finally pinpointed.

Doug unfolded an old island map, laying it flat on the picnic table. He carefully sketched the two subterranean channels, each one beginning at the shoreline and converging at the Money Pit.

"This second tunnel must be the one they dynamited in 1897," Doug said. "The echo analysis is a mess. The image doesn't resemble the other tunnel until we get to where it's 15 metres beneath the surface. But this is definitely it." He pointed on the map.

The location of the two tunnels had been carefully staked out on the ground based on echo-resonance imagery readings.

"Jake, we did pick up some odd feedback at 26 metres, just off to the side of the second tunnel," Doug said.

"How so?" Jake asked.

"It's a duplicate sound. The tunnel pattern repeats itself at the deeper level." Doug explained.

"What does it mean?" Jake asked.

"I think it's just some sort of a sonic shadow, or echo, from the second one." Doug said.

"Is there a possibility of a third tunnel?" Marion inquired.

"Not a chance," Doug said defensively. "The 1861 expedition dug up the entire beach and only found two. Incidentally, I haven't seen them yet, but I'm told several of the drillings contained traces of coconut husks."

"What's with the coconut husks?" I asked, having grown comfortable with these expedition discussions. "You mentioned them back home, too."

"Whoever made the flood tunnels covered the rocks with coconut fibres to keep the channels from getting clogged with dirt when they were reburied," Jake said.

"Basically, it was just a fibrous material in plentiful supply at the time," Marion added. "By the 1500s, explorers, merchant ships and even pirates used coconut fibres for packing cargo; the same way people use polystyrene foam today."

"It was one of the earliest clues that the pit was dug by a seafaring group," Jake said.

"So what now?" I asked. "How are you going to stop the sea water?"

Jake and Doug exchanged a smile.

"Get the team leaders together," Jake said. "It's time to break out the *goop*."

* * *

Jake held up a clear, 90-centimetre Plexiglas tube. Although wide enough for a softball to pass through, it had been tightly packed with gravel and rocks. A hose was attached to one end of the tube.

"This pipe represents a flood tunnel connecting the sea water reservoir to the pit. Until now, no one's been able to stop the flow of water," Jake explained. "They've tried digging them up, and as Doug pointed out, even dynamiting them, but to no avail — the water always finds a way through."

Jake set the pipe on the table at a downward sloping angle.

"Okay, Emma, turn on the hose," Jake instructed.

I turned the handle on the water tank. Moments later we could see the water flow through the rocks and gravel in the pipe, then out the other end and onto the ground.

"Until we stop the water," Jake said dramatically, gesturing to the water spilling out of the pipe, "we'll never get the treasure. The solution is goop."

"Goop?" I asked, anxious for this particular mystery to be solved.

"What's goop?" Marion asked.

"Let me explain," Jake said excitedly. "All the previous expeditions focused on digging up the tunnels — a huge, time-consuming task."

"And which, ironically, seems to have made the tunnels even bigger," Doug added.

"Rather than digging them up, we thought it might be easier to just clog them up with something," Jake said.

"Are you going to tell them that you got the idea when your kitchen drain got clogged?" Doug asked with a grin.

"I hadn't planned to," Jake said. "Anyway, there are several challenges to successfully clogging the channels. We need to pump something down there that can seep in-between all the rocks and fibres, while at the same time, harden underwater. That's how we came up with goop."

Doug handed Jake a metal pot that resembled the pressure cookers my grandmother used when she was canning vegetables. A hose at the top of the pot was attached to a portable air compressor. Another hose with a trigger nozzle came out the bottom of the pot. As Jake unclamped the lid, Doug entered the portable and returned with two steaming saucepans. Doug carefully poured the contents of the two saucepans into the pot and Jake quickly resealed the lid.

One of the liquids was thin and black. The other was lumpy and a putrid-green colour. Together they smelled like rotten tomatoes.

"It'll take a few minutes for the pot to reach sufficient pressure," Jake said.

"So it works like hot wax?" Joel asked.

"Very much so," Jake said. "When hot candle drippings fall into cold water, they instantly form a solid. That's the principle."

"Why not just use wax?" one of the crew asked.

"Good question," Jake said. "Paraffin solidifies too quickly. It wouldn't have a chance to seep into all the small spaces in the flood tunnel."

"Would plastic work?" I asked. This was like a school

science project, only on a much more serious scale. But I knew some science. Plastic sounded like the way to go.

"That might have worked, but we would have run into another problem," Jake answered.

"Environmental," Doug said. "The government takes a dim view of pumping thousands of litres of hot plastic into the ground, considering it virtually never decomposes."

"Right, we needed a compound that could seep in-between all the rocks, quickly harden in water, but also decompose in several months," Jake said. "We worked with chemists from AgriChem Corporation. They actually invented the stuff, although they liked our name for it."

"Getting government permits was the longest part of the process," Doug said. "It seemed like we had to get every-body's approval; from the Environmental Protection Branch of Environment Canada to the Office of Aboriginal Affairs. We even had to register with the National Pollutant Release Inventory. The whole process took eight months."

"It's ready!" Jake said, reading the pressure gauge on top of the pot.

He placed the trigger nozzle into the dime-sized hole on top of the clear pipe, from which water was still running onto the ground.

As Jake squeezed the trigger, the dark-green goop began oozing into the pipe. We could see it gradually envelop the rocks inside; seeping deeper and spreading wider until the molasses-like substance created a plug about 20 centimetres long.

The water spilling from the tube began to ease, then

slowed to a trickle, and finally stopped altogether. The water backed up and began spraying out the end where the hose was attached.

"You can turn off the water now, Emma," Jake said.

We were all impressed.

"What's in this stuff?" Marion asked.

Jake broke off a large piece of hardened goop and passed it around. It felt like greasy rubber cement, was a black-green colour, and still had that rotten tomato odour.

"In order for the compound to be biodegradable, and meet government requirements, it had to be a organic," Jake explained. "It's a corn-starch compound combined with concentrated pectin. Only after they're mixed at 21 degrees celsius do they become goop. The perfect drain clog."

"I'm truly impressed!" Marion said, looking at the pressurized cooking pot.

"Surprised a couple of lunkheads like Jake and I could come up with this?" Doug asked.

"Well, yes. I mean, no," Marion stammered. "You know what I mean."

The entire camp was relaxed and optimistic over the next three days. Finding the cave drawings combined with the successful testing of Uncle Jake's goop created a confident atmosphere.

Crew members began to realize there was a real chance for success. Joel and I overheard numerous conversations of how this person or that person planned to spend their share of the ancient treasure.

When it came time to make some more goop, Joel and I

watched as the crew removed 30, 200-litre drums from beneath the off-limits tarp. Fifteen were orange with black stencilled lettering that read: *AgriChem — CS Extract (H-14)*. The remaining barrels were black with yellow lettering: *AgriChem — Pbase Concentrate (H-53)*. Together, they could create more than 6,000 litres of goop. A large Caterpillar tractor was fitted with steel brackets to firmly hold two barrels. Each of the ingredients was slowly drained into a mixing and heating tank on the side of the tractor. With the pressurized hoses running out the front, I thought the customized tractor resembled some sort of weird mechanical beast. Once the heating tank was full, we were ready for what the crew called the *drill-it and fill-it* process.

Because it was important to completely block each flood tunnel, Jake insisted that the crew inject twice the amount of goop that Doug thought necessary. The process was simple — drill down 15 metres, insert the pressure hoses, then pump the hot, smelly mixture into the channels. Doug told us the drill-it and fill-it procedure was going to be repeated 15 times per tunnel in an overlapping pattern. Nearly 2,300 litres of goop would be pressure pumped into each of the two subterranean waterways. Each tunnel would take about 30 hours to clog, so the work was divided into 10-hour shifts.

Since the excavation work on the pit couldn't proceed until all the tunnels were clogged, Joel and I had plenty of time to ourselves. We beachcombed along the island's rocky coastline in the warm sun, made makeshift forts of driftwood, and explored the island's wooded interior. It was our own private summer camp. I still had some bad moments when I was in my tent alone at night, but for the most part I was happier than I had been in a long while. I was able to enjoy the expedition, the island and the freedom both afforded.

When the clogging job was done, the leftover supply of goop proved too great a temptation for the crew. It wasn't long before the goop-related jokes began. The best by far was a stunt in which the entire camp must have participated. One morning, as Doug entered one of the green plastic portable outhouses and latched the door behind him, six crew members sprang to life in a well-rehearsed military-like exercise. Three separate goop hoses were inserted into the outhouse's sides, and about 50 litres of the fast-hardening slop were pumped inside. It took three crew members to hold the door shut to thwart Doug's escape efforts.

As the goop hardened, cementing Doug's feet and legs in place, the outhouse was slowly tilted on its side, and unceremoniously rolled down a small hill. Doug's cursing and threats were barely audible above the crew's roaring laughter. When Doug finally escaped, he was a good sport about the whole thing, although no one claimed responsibility to his face — just in case.

In contrast, when Marion awoke to find her shoes filled with the black-green substance, she turned red in the face with anger.

"You people are really juvenile," she shouted.

"C'mon, Marion, the crew just needs to cut loose every

once in a while," Jake said, laughing.

"Actually, Uncle Jake," I whispered, "it was me and Joel who put the goop in Marion's shoes."

"Don't worry about it, Em," he whispered back, "we all need to let off a little steam. There's plenty of hard work ahead."

Now that the flood tunnels had been repeatedly pumped with thousands of litres of goop, the channels were tested with flow sensors. The anxiously awaited results were always the same — the water from the beach had been completely blocked. Not a single drop was seeping through toward the pit. It appeared that Uncle Jake had eliminated the greatest obstacle to successfully retrieving the treasure, whatever it was.

9

Stone Sentinels

UNCLE Jake hadn't been kidding when he said we'd do our fair share of work. By assigning menial tasks to Joel and me, Jake's crew could focus on the critical job of digging farther down into the pit. And I didn't mind. It made me feel part of something important. It was late in the afternoon when Jake called us to the table around which he, Doug and Marion were seated.

"You two ready for another job?" Jake asked.

"I suppose so," I answered. We hadn't done much that morning.

"Good. This one will give you a little exercise," he smiled.

"Let me explain," Jake said. "During the expedition of 1897, four rock markers were discovered that supposedly form a large arrow, pointing to the site of the Money Pit. Doug's crew located them before we flew up here. Doug, show them the map."

Doug unfolded his map of the island with four small red marks indicating the rocks. They seemed to form an arrow pointing toward our campsite.

"We think it's more a matter of coincidence and wishful thinking. Mainly because the stones are all about half a kilometre apart."

"What do you mean wishful thinking?" Joel asked Jake.

"Joel, there's been a lot of treasure hunters up here. It wouldn't surprise me if someone found the rocks, placed only by nature, and fabricated a story around them to add to the island's mystery," Jake explained. "But with the film crew coming, I thought they'd like to get some footage of them. It does add to the folklore."

"What do you want us to do?" I asked.

"The rocks are all pretty badly overgrown with brush," Jake said. "What I'd like, and Doug will help, is for you to clear the brush away as much as possible. We want the photographer to get a good shot."

"There's one important thing to remember," Marion said sternly. "Whatever you do, don't move them in any way. If there is anything factual about them, their exact positioning could be critical."

"Relax, Marion," Doug said. "I've seen them. You'd need a winch to budge these things."

"I'll drop you and the tools off at what we call Rock No. 3," Doug instructed. "It sits on the edge of a ravine. Only one side is overgrown but you'll have your work cut out for you."

"Just be careful," Jake added. "The ravine drops off pretty steeply behind the rock."

"When you're done, meet me here at Rock No. 4," Doug said, pointing to the map. "This one has an old tree growing around it. I'll clear out the smaller stuff and wait until you get there to take it down. You think you'd like to try your hand with a chainsaw, Joel?"

"You mean it?" he asked excitedly.

"Sure. You'll make the first cut," Doug replied.

* * *

Doug pulled his old battered Jeep to a stop on the narrow dirt road. He pointed to a recently cut pathway through the brush.

"It's straight ahead about 100 metres, right where the trail ends. When you're done, just follow this little road. I'll park the Jeep on the side. You'll be able to see me from there."

"Okay," we said, pulling an axe, rake and brush cutter from the Jeep and waving as Doug drove off toward Rock No. 4.

It was surprising that Doug had been able to find the rock at all. It was almost completely hidden by huckleberry, holly and alder, most of it twice my height. The rock leaned slightly over the edge of the steep ravine. A small creek gurgled 15 metres below. Thankfully, just as Jake had said, there was very little brush against the rock on the ravine side. We'd only be clearing brush on level ground. The ravine itself was thickly blanketed with a mixture of sheep laurel, blueberry and alder bushes.

It was hard work. Joel cut the bigger bushes with the axe, and I dragged them to a pile. Several times while we were working, I had the strangest feeling we were being watched. It was a tingly feeling on the back of my neck. But each time I stopped and looked around, there was never anyone there. Just the same, I had a strong suspicion we weren't alone.

After two hours of hot, sweaty work, we'd cleared the brush from around the rock. Now we could better examine it. The tall, thin rock jutted about one-and-a-half metres from the ground. There didn't look to be anything very special about it. One side was flat and moss covered, while the other was jagged and irregular. Joel leaned against it, absentmindedly pulling off the moss.

"Look, Em," he said. "Zorro was here!"

On the flat side of the rock, underneath the moss, ran a vein of white quartz making the shape of a large "Z."

"Very funny," I said, wiping the sweat from my forehead and temples. After two hours of cutting and hauling brush I'd lost my sense of humour. I was tired and dirty and wanted to get back to camp.

"Let's find Doug," Joel suggested. "He's got a cooler in the Jeep with drinks."

"Good idea!" A pop was an excellent idea. So was a shower, but that wasn't going to be happening soon.

As we walked back through the thickly wooded trail I was sure I saw something move behind a tree far off to our side. I ducked down out of sight and signalled Joel to do the same.

"What's up?" he asked in a whisper.

We were down on all fours, hidden by brush.

"Somebody's watching us. Over there!" I said, pointing to two large trees. "I think I saw a face between those trees."

"You stay here and make them think I'm still here," Joel said. I'll sneak back around and see who it is."

"Be careful," I said, sounding a bit too much like our mother.

"No sweat! No one can outrun me in the woods. Just in case, I'll take this with me." He picked up a large rock.

Joel silently crawled back down the trail. I stood to do my part.

"Well, I thought it was an ant hill!" I said loud enough to be overheard. "Come on, Joel, stop fooling around. We've got to get going!"

Joel slipped effortlessly into the brush without the slightest noise. He circled around toward the large trees I had indicated. Back home we had a lot of woods around our house and we played with the neighbourhood kids, trying to sneak up on one another. I don't remember Joel ever losing; not once.

"Joel!" I shouted to the vacant ground. "Leave those bugs alone! Doug's expecting us and he'll come looking for us if we're late!"

Joel moved in slow motion. He thoughtfully placed his feet so as to avoid branches, dry twigs, loose rocks and logs. He moved silently and fluidly. Finally he paused when only one tall bush separated him from the two trees. Slowly he leaned around the bush, raised the rock, and prepared to strike. But there was nothing there!

"False alarm," he called to me. "There's no one here!"

I stopped my imaginary conversation and went to see for myself.

"It was probably just a bird or something," Joel said.

"Would a bird do that?" I said pointing to the ground.

The tall grass had been trampled behind the trees.

"Did you do that?" I asked.

"No! I came up from the other side," Joel explained. "I'm not a klutz, you know."

"Then someone was definitely here."

"That's impossible! I didn't see anything," Joel protested. "I would have at least heard them."

"Well, someone was standing here," I concluded. "And they're certainly not here now!"

After returning to the trail, we found Doug in a small clearing. Rock No. 4 didn't look much different from our own No. 3. It stuck out of the ground and was just a little bit shorter. However, a large fir tree, nearly a metre in diameter, had grown up around the rock. The stone was practically embedded in the tree's rough bark. Thick roots encircled the base of the stone. The tree abruptly ended 10 metres overhead, the victim of either lightning or a severe windstorm.

"How did it go?" Doug asked.

"Fine," I answered. "We cleared everything away from it."

"Good! Joel, are you ready for a lesson?" Doug asked, pointing to the bright yellow chainsaw near the tree.

"Definitely!" Joel said.

Joel put on safety goggles and Doug explained how the saw worked, how to start it and, most importantly, how to hold it.

"This is *really* heavy!" Joel said with surprise.

"We need a big one for a tree this size," Doug said. "The blade has to reach all the way through the trunk."

Joel pulled the starter cord and the engine roared to life. It was deafening! He squeezed the trigger beneath the handle and the chain's sharp teeth disappeared in a terrifying blur, spinning around the long shaft. Doug helped Joel make one downward, slanting cut into the trunk just above the rock. Then Doug took the saw to finish the job.

Doug explained that the idea was to cut out a wedge, halfway through the tree, on the side where you wanted it to fall. Then, on the other side, above and behind the wedge, cut down diagonally. As the saw bit deeper into the trunk, the tree would fall where it had the least support — where the wedge piece was missing. It sounded easy until Doug turned and shouted at us before making the final cut.

"You two get back out of the way. These things never fall where I want them to!"

A shower of sawdust accompanied the high-speed saw. The dead tree wavered for an instant, then fell to the ground with a crash.

"I need your help over here," Doug called to us. "I'll cut the stump off at the ground. Push hard against it while I'm cutting so it doesn't pinch the saw and jam the chain."

We leaned against the tall stump as Doug worked the deafening chainsaw through the base. We could feel the stump begin to give. As he cut through the last fibres, it toppled. For the first time in perhaps several hundred years, the rock was free.

"Good work!" Doug shouted. Even though he'd shut off the saw, the sound kept ringing in my ears. "I don't know about you two, but I'm getting hungry for dinner. I'll take the saw and wedges back to the Jeep if you can carry the other tools."

Doug lifted the saw as if it was a feather and began to trudge back to the Jeep. Joel and I gathered up the other tools.

"Joel!" I called.

"What?"

"Come here," I said. "Hurry!"

He dropped the tools and ran to my side.

"What's the matter?"

"Look!" I said pointing to the rock.

On the flat side of the rock, which had been hidden by the tree's massive trunk, was a thin line of white quartz in the unmistakable mirror image of a "Z."

10

Divitias

WE didn't tell Doug about the stones. We never had the chance.

"Hurry up!" he called. "We've got to get back to camp. Your uncle's up to his butt in alligators!"

He was waiting for us beside his Jeep looking worried. He had just talked with Marion on the two-way radio. The instant we climbed into our seats, Doug stomped on the gas pedal. The old Jeep practically flew down the bumpy road. It didn't do much for my aching muscles.

"What's wrong?" Joel shouted above the engine's whine. "Is someone hurt?"

Joel and I bounced off our seats and banged our heads on the padded roll bar as we ran over a large bump.

"Get those seat belts on!" Doug ordered. "No one's hurt."

"So what's wrong?" I asked, figuring it must be pretty serious, but hoping it wasn't.

Doug slowed down a bit so we could hear each other.

"The most important thing for a big expedition like this is money," he explained. "The equipment, the crew, supplies, transportation — it's expensive. Your uncle and I could never afford all of it. The money comes from investors. If we find treasure, the investors get a share of it. If the treasure's big, then the investors make a lot of money.

"Two investors are backing out and Jake's got to figure out how to cover the shortfall. Unless he can convince them to stay with us, we're out of money!"

"Will we have to quit?" I asked. I almost didn't want to hear the answer, because I couldn't imagine all of this coming to such a bitter end. I looked at Joel and he looked worried, too.

"Jake never quits!" Doug smiled. "He's not the quitting kind. He'll figure out something. He always does. I'm just sorry he has to deal with this."

We got to camp in record time. Doug immediately jumped out and rushed into the main tent. We tried to follow, but Marion stopped us outside.

"Sorry guys," she said. "Your uncle's on a pretty intense call. He said no interruptions; not even for you. You may as well get yourself some dinner. He's likely to be tied up for several hours."

Reluctantly, we left the main tent and headed to dinner. It was the first opportunity Joel and I had to talk about the stone markers.

"Both rocks have the exact same 'Z' shapes; both on the flat side," I quietly said to Joel. We didn't want to be overheard. I was fairly certain we had made another major discovery, but I wanted to hear Joel's opinion. With all the trouble, this was no time to be sending people on wild goose chases.

"Joel, it must be the same rock! Somebody split it in half! Someone went to a huge amount of trouble to put the rocks in those exact positions. It's not coincidence. They point to the treasure! The stones are real!"

"So what now?" Joel said.

"If the stones were put there by whoever buried the treasure, maybe there are artifacts buried around them."

"Artifacts?" Joel asked.

"You know," I explained. "Maybe an old tool, or a coin, or a knife; anything they may have dropped."

"You're saying we dig one up?" Joel said a little too loudly.

"Shhh! We'll just dig around it," I said. "If we don't find anything we'll just come back and tell Jake about them."

"I suppose so," Joel said tentatively. "When?"

"Tonight. As soon as everyone falls asleep."

It was past 11 p.m. when we silently crept out of camp with a shovel and rake and crept up the trail-like road. Other than a dim light in Uncle Jake's tent, all the tents were dark. It was a clear night. The moon flooded the area in silver light, casting sinister, harsh black shadows. We didn't need flashlights until we turned onto the small trail that went off into the woods.

We found the stone we'd cleared earlier in the day, No. 3, overlooking the deep ravine. Just as we were whispering our plan to one another, a blood-chilling howl echoed through the darkness from far away.

"Jeez!" Joel gasped in a loud whisper. "Is that what you heard the other night?"

"Yes, that's definitely it," I said, glancing around nervously.

"Jake didn't say anything about wolves or coyotes," Joel said.

"I don't hear anything now." I was desperately trying to listen beyond the leaves rustling overhead in the breeze.

"Come on," Joel said. "Let's get this over with as fast as possible."

Joel carefully dug around the base of the stone. As he removed each shovelful of dirt, I raked it in search of clues or artifacts. After an hour Joel had completely unearthed the large rock. It looked eerie in the silver moonlight. We had made a large dirt pile, but had discovered nothing. Exhausted, Joel climbed out of the hole and leaned against the cool surface of the rock to catch his breath.

"Well that was a complete waste of time," he said looking at his blistered hands.

"And now we've got to fill it in again."

"Sorry," I said, feeling silly. "It seemed like a good idea. I'll rake the dirt back..."

"Aagh!" Joel suddenly cried out.

The stone teetered over the side of the ravine with Joel holding on tightly. It shot down the steep bank, over the slippery leaves, like a runaway bobsled. Joel's cries echoed through the forest as the heavy stone plunged toward the creek. It smashed into the stream bed with a loud CRACK! Joel flew through the air, over the narrow stream, and landed face down in the dirt. The stone settled sideways in the creek, the slow-running water gurgling lazily around it.

When I shook off my shock enough to move, I carefully picked my way down the slippery hillside as fast as I could. Joel slowly stood up and brushed himself off.

"Are you okay?" I called.

"Did you see that, Em?" he said excitedly. "What a ride! That was better than Disneyland! Did you see it? How fast do you think I was going?"

"Is that all you can say?" I shouted. "Do you have any idea how much trouble we're in? Remember what Marion said — 'Whatever you do, don't move the rock!'"

"It's worse than that, Em," he said. "Look at it."

"Oh no!"

I couldn't believe our bad luck. A huge chunk had broken off the top of the rock when it crashed into the stones along the creek.

"You broke it!" I said, smacking my filthy forehead. "We're toast!"

"It's not my fault!" Joel shouted back.

"Well, it's not mine!" I said, pretty sure I hadn't been the one to lean on the rock with enough force to send it tumbling.

"Uncle Jake's going to *kill* us when he sees this!" he said.

"At least the bottom isn't smashed," I said. I turned on my flashlight and pointed its bright beam along the length of the long rock.

"Em, point the light back at the bottom," Joel said.

The flat bottom of the stone was caked with thick dirt. The water had washed some of it away, revealing some sort of markings. Joel waded into the creek and furiously splashed water onto the rock's base to wash away more soil. As the dirt gradually washed away, the markings slowly became visible. Crudely chiselled onto the underside of the rock were the letters: D-I-V-I-T-I-A-S.

Once we explained the markings to Uncle Jake, things happened fast, even though it was the middle of the night. In less than an hour, he awoke his entire crew to dig up the three remaining stones. Just as we suspected, each stone had cryptic lettering carved onto the bottom. I'd never seen everyone in camp so excited! Our disaster had turned into something quite the opposite, luckily for us.

It was one o'clock in the morning when Jake, Doug, Marion, Joel and I clustered around the white board in the main tent. In front of us were the letters, or words, secretly hidden under the stone markers for hundreds of years:

DIVITIAS
PETE
REGNI
EIUS

"It looks like some sort of code," Jake said solemnly.

"Maybe it's a letter scramble," I suggested, feeling some ownership in the puzzle. "You know, where the letters are all mixed up."

"Do the words mean anything backwards?" Joel asked.

"They don't appear to," Uncle Jake said thoughtfully.

"You're all just guessing!" Marion said. "Listen, I've got a friend at Dalhousie University with an advanced degree in mathematics. He has access to a Cray supercomputer. He claims he can break any code within 24 hours. I'll call him tomorrow morning and we'll have the answer by..."

"We can solve this in 30 seconds," Doug interrupted.

"What!" Marion stammered. "How?"

"It's Latin guys," Doug said calmly.

"I think you're right!" Jake said. "It sure sounds like it."

"Anybody here know Latin?" Doug asked.

His question was met with silence.

"Wait a minute!" I said. "I know a Web site that translates different languages into English. I use it for school."

"Marion, can you get us a connection?" Jake asked.

"Already working on it," Marion answered as she opened her laptop and connected the satellite phone to it.

I gave Marion the Web address. This site could translate 40 different languages — including Latin.

"Okay," Marion said. "Let's see if this is it. What's the first word?"

"DIVITIAS," Jake said.

We all peered over Marion's shoulder at the small screen as she entered the letters. The five of us held our breath as we watched the hourglass icon, waiting for an answer. Then a word flashed across the screen: wealth.

"It is Latin!" I shouted.

Marion entered the other words, each quickly translated. Doug wrote them on the white board:

DIVITIAS = WEALTH
PETE = SEEK

REGNI = KINGDOM
EIUS = HIS

"Fantastic!" Jake said. "This is incredible! It does look like a word scramble."

Marion adjusted her glasses.

"Four different words means there are 24 different variations..." she began.

"Seek...His...Kingdom's...Wealth," Joel slowly uttered. We all looked over to Joel, then back at the words.

"Seek His Kingdom's Wealth," Jake slowly repeated. "I think he's right!"

"Amazing!" Doug stammered.

"Okay, guys," Jake said, rubbing his bloodshot eyes. "We need to get a historical analysis of this and we don't have much time!"

"I can run an Internet search tonight and research all the possibilities," Marion volunteered.

"Thanks Marion," Jake said appreciatively.

"If you don't mind," Doug added, "I'd like to work with you on this. I don't know how much I can help — it's more a matter of curiosity."

"I welcome the help," Marion said.

"You kids need to get some sleep. We'll have the results in the morning," Jake said. "I think you have more than earned your keep on this one!"

"Jake, you look like you could use a little sleep yourself," Doug observed. "You've had enough to worry about today."

"I wouldn't mind a little shut-eye," he admitted.
"Okay," Doug said. "Let's get to work! Let's see what we can come up with by morning."

11

Two Thousand Kilos of Gold

MOST people considered my uncle nothing more than an empty-headed promoter. But Jake took this business seriously and he ran his meetings with military precision. It was *all* business. Behind the scenes, the overly confident, can-do personality rarely emerged, but there was never the slightest doubt about who was in charge.

Marion and Doug approached the table where Jake, Joel and I were already seated. Marion booted up her laptop to open the files she'd downloaded off the Internet the night before.

"Okay," Jake began. "Let's see if we can figure this out before we announce the stone markers to the press. Marion, what did you find?"

We hoped the inscriptions would help pin down exactly who dug the pit, and what it might contain. Jake explained that if we knew what was down there, we'd know what salvage methods to avoid in case it was something extremely fragile.

"I'm not sure it's what you're looking for," Marion said.

"There must be at least one match!" Jake said with a hint of irritation.

"That's not the problem," Marion explained. "There are too many possibilities!"

"Doesn't the Latin narrow it down?" Jake asked.

"Irrelevant," Marion said flatly. "Latin was a second language to every educated person for the period we're considering. Except..."

"Except what?" Jake asked.

"Marion and I spoke about this last night," Doug said, entering the conversation. "Latin was a second language to everyone who might have done this, except pirates."

I could see Uncle Jake didn't like that. Pirate treasure had always been his pet theory and this fact eliminated the pirate theory from consideration.

"What about the cave?" he asked.

Marion and Doug looked at each other and shrugged their shoulders.

"I guess we can't explain it, Jake," Marion confessed.

"All right. What *do* we have?" Jake asked Marion.

Marion referred back to her computer.

"I ran an analysis from 1500 through 1800, just to cover all our bases. I combined geographic relevance, with any country with credible nautical or navigational capabilities that had a male monarch, or king, during this period," Marion explained. "I cross-referenced that with any major loss of treasure the monarch experienced — gold, diamonds, jewels, anything for whatever reason."

"Well?" Jake asked. We were all eager to hear the results.

"Okay, I think France is out," Marion concluded. "It had a long succession of kings, and several explorers in this region, most notably Cartier in 1541, Champlain in 1604 and LaSalle in 1668, but it wasn't until the French Revolution in 1789 that Louis XVI had an enormous amount of jewels disappear."

"He also lost his head, as I recall," Doug added.

"Maybe that's what's buried down there," Marion grinned.

"Let's stay focused guys," Jake said with authority.

"Would the pit have been dug that late?" I asked.

"Emma's right," Jake confirmed. "We're looking for something much earlier. What else have you got?"

"Between 1706 and 1750, under John V, the Portuguese brought shiploads of gold back from Brazil. On one expedition, two ships were lost at sea," Marion read from her screen. "It was assumed they were sunk by storms or attacked by pirates. Assuming one of the pirates spoke Latin, I think that has to be considered a possibility."

"Doug?" Jake asked.

"It would fit," Doug added. "Just the language issue."

"When specifically did the ships go down?" Jake asked.

"I've got conflicting dates. Either 1736 or 1737," Marion answered. "I'd have to make a few phone calls to pin it down."

Jake's scowl told us that he thought something was wrong.

"Are all these correlations from the 1700s?" Jake asked.

Marion looked up, carefully adjusting her glasses. Marion always did that before she was going say anything she thought was important. It was a little signal that we were all to listen carefully.

"Jake, these are all possibilities. All the previous carbon dating has been grossly inaccurate. We all need to keep an open mind to the possible time frame."

"All right professor," Jake said yielding to Marion's superior historical knowledge. "I'll try to keep my prejudices in check. Keep going."

"We've got two possibilities for England. In 1758, the English captured Louisbourg from the French. There was looting, but no one knows exactly what was taken or what happened to it." Marion paused to make several entries into the computer. "After that, in 1762, the British captured Havana, Cuba, from the Spanish. Again, they took a tremendous amount of gold coin as well as the traditional spoils of war. Yet there is no record as to what happened to the money."

"None of those would seem to tie in strongly with a particular king," Jake challenged.

"Agreed," Marion said. "Although they're within the realm of possibility, I think they're both pretty weak."

"Let's not forget there were a lot of settlers living in Nova Scotia in the 1700s," Jake pointed out. "I tend to believe that any large-scale excavation during the second half of the eighteenth century would have left some record with the residents. But we don't have that! I still believe it was earlier. Marion, what about the Italians?"

"No good matches," Marion said. "Vespucci arrived in Brazil in 1501 but he didn't go far enough inland to find anything. Verrazano was the first to sail into New York harbour in 1524, but again no riches."

"The Dutch?" Jake asked.

"Pretty much the same thing," Marion answered. "Henry Hudson sailed under the Dutch flag in 1609 trying to discover the Northwest Passage, but the expedition was a failure. They also didn't really have a king until the 1800s."

"How about the Spanish?" Jake said.

Marion leaned forward intently.

"There's several possibilities but one really stands out," she said. "I think you're going to like it, Jake. In 1532, Francisco Pizarro was returning home from Peru after the virtual genocide of the Incas."

"And you thought it wasn't pirates," Doug added.

"Much worse in this case," Jake said.

"This was during the reign of Charles V," Marion continued. "Well, they returned to Spain with 4,000 kilos of gold — a sizeable amount. However, historians estimate that they stole *6,000* kilos of gold from the capital city of Cuzco."

"What happened to the other 2,000 kilos?" I asked.

"Pizarro could easily have made a detour to Oak Island and buried the gold, thinking he would retrieve it later." Marion leaned back with a slight grin, looking across the table to Jake.

"I can tell by that smug expression that you're holding something back," Jake observed.

"The Spanish got the gold by ransoming the Incan Emperor Atahualpa. It was the wealth of his entire kingdom," Marion said in a hushed tone. *"His kingdom's wealth."*

"Doug?" Jake asked, seeking a second opinion.

"Two thousand kilos, that's ... just shy of $30 million," Doug tapped out the figures on a calculator. "But it's too early, Jake. It wasn't until 1600 that the Europeans had the air-pumping technology that would allow them to dig a narrow pit 38 metres straight down. There wouldn't have been sufficient air exchange. The workers would have been asphyxiated before they got past 27 metres."

"Wait a minute, Doug," Jake interrupted. "The trenches started at the beach, right? Here on the windward side of the island?"

"Yes..." Doug slowly answered.

"I see what you mean," I jumped in. "If the trenches started shallow and gradually got deeper, wouldn't the wind blowing off the beach blow through the trenches and give them fresh air?"

"It's an interesting idea, Emma, but I think it's kind of a reach," Doug said. "I wouldn't have bet my life on it."

"The workers who dug this may not have had a choice," Jake said.

"So who was it?" Joel asked, cutting straight to the point, as usual.

"Good question." Jake said, "Guys?"

"In theory," Marion began, "*any* of these scenarios are within the realm of possibility."

"They all seem like long shots to me, Jake," Doug stated. "There just isn't enough supporting data."

"Right, but one of these long shots, one of these implausible scenarios actually occurred," Jake said. He stood up and began pacing, returning to his more charismatic self. "You're all missing the most important point! We have proof! Between this and the cave drawing we have two pieces of physical evidence from the time the treasure was buried.

"It's no longer a matter of conjecture. Centuries ago a tremendous treasure was buried here. It's down there, waiting for us to bring it to the surface!"

12

Ten Metres to Go

THE ninth support section swung momentarily above the depths of the pit, then gradually began a carefully controlled descent. We had reached 28 metres. By all accounts, the goop was still working. Each load of black-brown dirt hauled to the surface was examined to assess its moisture level. It was damp, and its wetness was increasing the deeper we went, but not enough to halt our progress.

A remote video camera, light and microphone accompanied all the workers into the pit. We were able to monitor their progress and it provided another measure of safety. Doug was watching the distorted images on his laptop. Joel and I sat nearby, not wanting to miss a thing. Far from being pesky little kids in the way, the crew treated us like valued members of the team, members who had made a couple of significant finds, and offered a couple of valuable ideas.

We could see the structural section slide inside the eighth support piece — Beth Rabel and Joseph Ibrahim, the two *moles* on this shift, locked it into place with the same type of pressure clamps used to secure the eight sections above.

"That's the last seal," Beth said, tightening the final

pressure clamp. The computer's small speaker made her voice tinny.

Beth and Joseph both wore grey, dirt-covered jumpsuits, heavy work boots and hard hats. Despite the sophisticated equipment on the surface, deep in the bowels of the pit, earth had to be removed the same way it was 200 years ago — shovel by shovel.

"Only an hour left," Beth said, glancing at her watch. "I'll be glad to get out of here."

Joseph handed her a shovel.

"I take it you've lost your taste for underground work?" he said.

"It didn't bother me at first," she said, digging her shovel into the bottom of the pit. "But the work space is getting smaller and smaller. I'm sick of the halogen lights, sick of the incessant pumping sound..."

"We've got to have breathable air," Joseph observed.

"I know," Beth agreed. "It's not just that. It's always wearing this stupid harness and being repeatedly raised and lowered like a yo-yo. If I wanted to spend my life like this I would have become a miner. Doesn't it ever get to you?"

"Not the work so much," Joseph answered. "This is my third expedition. I can put up with tough conditions, even the poor food, which is the worst I've ever had on a project like this. But a lot of us are fed up with all the stalling and excuses about our pay."

On the surface, we shifted around as the conversation headed in an uncomfortable direction, which we couldn't help but overhear.

"Yeah, what's up with that?" Beth asked.

"The night crew's convinced Morgan's got serious financial problems. I've heard quite a few of them are thinking about quitting," Joseph said.

Doug finally interrupted their conversation, switching on his microphone.

"Hey guys, if you're going to whine, don't do it when I'm watching and listening," Doug said.

"Sorry," Joseph said sincerely, looking into the camera.

"We'll talk about this later," Doug said sternly.

Well, good, I thought. If they were going to talk about Jake behind his back they deserved whatever Doug had in mind for them. He's got enough to deal with without trouble in the crew, I thought. He was good to them, and they should appreciate that.

Beth's shovel made a loud clank as it hit something.

"Hang on," she said. "I've got something here. Sounds like metal."

Beth got down on her knees and started carefully digging with her hands. We could see a rusted metal bar, sticking straight up out of the ground. She pulled more dirt away from the protruding object until 30 centimetres of it was revealed, the rest of it still deeply buried.

"Can you tell what it is?" Joseph asked.

"A $750 finder's bonus for me," she said with a smile.

"Seriously," Joseph insisted.

"No," Beth answered. "I've no idea what it is."

* * *

Once word got out that something had been discovered, most of the crew converged around the pit. Beth and Joseph, having already been hoisted to the surface and still in their safety harnesses, stood on the edge of the shaft. Joel and I stood near Jake, inside the safety perimeter.

"Where did they say they found it?" Jake shouted to Doug above the roar of the crane's engine.

"Between 28 and 29 metres," Doug shouted back. "It was sticking straight out of the ground toward the edge of the hole."

The metal bar emerged from the pit secured to a portable stretcher intended for injured workers. The motor ceased once the stretcher was safely on the ground. The bar was one-and-a-half metres long and four centimetres in diameter, and tapered at one end. It was swollen and blistered with rust and corrosion. A thick chunk had broken off where Beth struck it with her shovel. The interior was dark black.

"Was there anything underneath it?" Jake asked Beth.

"It was resting on rotten wood," Beth said. "I'm not sure how large the platform area is. We only dug down around the bar."

Jake carefully grasped the bar with both hands, and gingerly lifted it to gauge its weight.

"I figured about 20 kilograms," Beth said.

"I'd say you were about right," Jake agreed.

"What is it?" Beth asked.

"You thinking what I'm thinking?" Jake asked Doug.

"An iron bar, 30 metres down; it has to be," Doug replied.

"You're looking at what started it all," Jake said to the

assembled group. "In 1804, the Onslow Company successfully reached this level, just shy of 31 metres. They had encountered another platform of oak logs, similar to all those above. It was nightfall — quitting time. But before being pulled from the pit, Thomas Gilford, one of the workers, thought he would pry up several of the logs to get a head start on the next day's work. He drove *this* bar between the logs and pried one away from the others.

"Writing in his journal, that same night, he described a suction noise when he had moved the log, followed by a faint gurgling sound. Anyway, the rest of the crew was anxious for supper and forced him to stop. He was hoisted out of the pit, leaving his pry bar behind. The rest is history.

"At daybreak they discovered the pit was flooded. Gilford had unknowingly broken a seal holding back sea water," Jake concluded.

I know it's silly to feel sorry for a piece of metal, but looking down at the old pry bar, I felt we had finally brought it back to the surface where it belonged.

"You know," Marion observed, "In a way, if it wasn't for this, someone else would have already recovered the treasure. Mr. Gilford did us a favour."

"True enough," Doug agreed.

"This is a historic moment," Jake said to us. "No one's gotten this far before. From here on, anything we find won't be from prior expeditions. It will be from the group that actually buried the treasure. We've only 10 metres left — that's all! In just a few short days we'll be opening one of the richest treasures of our time."

But I still wondered what the treasure chest held — Incan gold, French jewels, pirate loot, or English spoils of war? Whatever it was, the end of the mystery was close at hand.

13

Father Langley

UNCLE Jake and Doug invited Joel and me on the drive back along the shore to Chester.

Once in town, Joel and I ate lunch at an outdoor café while Jake and Doug completed some personal business. They met us back at the restaurant just as we were finishing our hamburgers. Jake asked us to wait so he and Doug could compare the results of their respective errands. They moved several tables away for privacy, but we could faintly hear them.

"How'd it go?" Jake asked Doug in a conspiratorial tone.

"Not so good," Doug quietly answered. "Once word got out that we were trying to unload stuff, everybody knew we were in trouble. The few things I was able to sell were for a fraction of what they're worth."

"I'm not surprised," Jake said.

"If we could just sell one of the bigger pieces of equipment…" Doug began.

"You know it's not ours to sell," Jake said. "It's all rented. It all goes back to Halifax once this is over."

"How'd you do?" Doug asked.

"Not much better," Jake replied. "I got as much cash as possible from my credit cards, even cashed in my airline ticket back home."

"Jake, you shouldn't have done that!"

"We need enough money for food and to pay the crew part of what we owe them," Jake said in a loud whisper. "We've got to convince them to hang in there just a little longer. We can't have them walk off the job when we're so close!"

"I'm sorry I can't do more personally to help," Doug said looking down.

"Don't even think it," Jake said. "You have a family to support — I don't. Besides, we're going to do it this time, Doug. I've never been so sure of it. We've only got 10 metres left to go."

"This is the worst cash squeeze we've ever had," Doug said. "It's a miracle we've managed for this long."

"We'll get through it," Jake said confidently. "Just so long as the crew gets paid. They've risked a lot coming up here. Most of them can't afford to go home empty-handed."

Jake glanced in our direction. We kept our eyes down, not wanting them to know we understood the gravity of the situation. I was beginning to think that despite all that had happened to me, Uncle Jake's luck was actually worse than mine.

"One other thing, Doug," he said quietly. "The kids know we've got money problems, but I'd prefer it if you don't mention to them about me selling my stuff."

I could see that Jake was ashamed of the situation.

"I understand," Doug nodded.

"Anyway, once we raise the chest we'll never have to worry about money again!" Jake said returning to his optimistic self.

"I hope you're right," Doug said.

Joel and I didn't notice that a man had approached our table until he was standing next to us.

"Good afternoon," he said, making Joel and I jump with surprise.

"Hello," I said looking up at him with a slightly wrinkled, freckled and sunburned nose.

The man, in his mid-20s, was clean shaven and had thick brown hair. He wore a short-sleeve black shirt and an old-fashioned priest's collar.

"I didn't mean to startle you," he said. "My name is Daniel Langley."

"Emma. And this is Joel."

"You're a priest?" Joel asked. His directness could be downright rude.

"Yes, that's correct," Langley answered.

"I thought priests were all really old," Joel said.

"Joel!" I said, kicking him under the table with enough force to get my point across.

"It's true, I'm not very old," Langley said leaning down so that he was face-to face with Joel. "But it won't take long, just a few years, and then I'll be as old as the hills."

Joel laughed nervously and Father Langley gave us both a disarming smile. I was glad he wasn't offended by my little brother's immaturity.

"I see that you're with Jake Morgan," Langley said. "Is he your father?"

"No, he's our uncle," I replied.

"I admire him tackling the Money Pit. It's a formidable challenge. How is the project proceeding?" Langley asked.

"We're really close! He thinks we may be able to get the treasure in a few days," I answered, unsure how much I should reveal.

"Remarkable!" Langley said thoughtfully. "After so many centuries we'll finally learn what's buried down there."

"We're pretty sure it's pirate treasure; a humongous chest of gold!" Joel said with great authority.

"*Humongous?*" Langley smiled.

"Actually," I corrected Joel, "a lot of the clues point to gold the Spanish took from the Incan Empire."

"I'd like to believe that such great effort was a result of faith, rather than solely for money," Father Langley said.

"What do you mean?" Joel asked.

"Well, there are many theories as to what lies at the bottom of the pit," he explained. "One theory holds that it's the Holy Grail and the Crown of Thorns."

"*The* Crown of Thorns, from Jesus, here in Nova Scotia?" I didn't do a very good job of hiding my disbelief.

"I know it sounds far-fetched," Father Langley smiled. "May I sit with you for a moment?"

"Sure," Joel said agreeably. Father Langley sat down at our table.

"Do you both understand the significance of these sacred artifacts?" he asked.

"The Crown of Thorns was put on Jesus when he was crucified," I said.

"And the Grail is the cup from the Last Supper," Joel added. "Everyone knows that!"

"That's correct. But let me tell you some things that not quite so many people know," Father Langley said in a hushed tone. His eyes had a fiery intensity to them as he began to speak. I moved in closer so I wouldn't miss a word.

"Although the crown was referred to and spoken of in early Christian teachings, there was no specific knowledge of its actual location. Then a reference was discovered in the writings of St. Paulinus of Nola. He claims to have seen the crown while in Jerusalem in 409 AD."

Father Langley signalled the waiter to bring him a glass of water.

"This was substantiated by another reference, discovered in the notes of Antonius of Piacenze who viewed the crown 90 years later in the Church at Mount Sion, again in Jerusalem. There are no other known references to the crown's location again until 870 AD when a pious monk named Bernard wrote of his pilgrimage to the Church at Mount Sion. He, too, was shown the crown. But in 1063 AD, the Crown of Thorns was to be transferred from Jerusalem to Byzantium. This is where the historical controversy begins," Father Langley said.

"Controversy?" I asked.

"While the crown was being transported to the Eastern Empire, the caravan was attacked. Many of the escorts were killed. Amazingly, the case containing the crown was undisturbed. At the time, it was assumed the raid had been the work of armed bandits, ignorant of the value of the precious cargo. And because the Eastern Empire attached only minor significance to the crown, the box containing it remained sealed. The box's contents were never inspected. In 1238 AD, 175 years later, Baldwin II, the Latin emperor of Constantinople, needing a strong ally, offered the crown to Louis, king of France," Langley explained.

"But when the case was finally opened in Paris, it contained only a circle of rushes, or reeds — no thorns!"

"What happened?" Joel asked.

"Ancient writings revealed that when the original caravan was attacked leaving Jerusalem, each of the attackers had a red cross upon their shields. Historians now know this was the insignia of the Knights Templar," Father Langley said dramatically.

"Knights Templar?" I asked. "Who are they?"

"The Knights Templar was a secret order of knights, originally formed to protect the Crusaders and their families on the road to the Holy Land. However, the sect became more and more extreme in their religious views, and more and more obsessed with secrecy. They became quite fanatical," Langley said. "Little is really known about them."

Uncle Jake, standing nearby, used the break in Father Langley's tale to approach the table. Father Langley abruptly stood up.

"I'm sorry," Father Langley apologized to Jake. "I didn't mean to delay the children."

"No, no, please," Jake said, urging Langley to sit back down. "I didn't realize you were such a historian."

"An amateur historian to be sure," he replied modestly.

"You seem to have many talents. I heard that you are also a volunteer medic with the fire department," Jake observed.

"One does what one must in a small community," Langley replied.

"Sounds like you save people one way or another," Jake joked.

"I'll take that as a compliment," Langley smiled. The two shook hands.

"Please continue your story," Jake urged. "Your audience is on the edge of its seats!"

Jake took an empty chair from a nearby table and sat between Joel and me as Father Langley sat down.

"Well, as I was saying," Father Langley began, "many historical scholars believe it was the Knights Templar who attacked the caravan, seized the true Crown of Thorns, and replaced it with the reeds that went undiscovered for almost 200 years."

"Is that true?" I asked Jake.

"Shhh," he answered. "I think Father Langley has more to tell."

"Well, yes." Langley said. "As to the Holy Grail, there's a little more conjecture involved."

"Conjecture?" Joel asked.

"Guessing!" I said.

"In the 1890s, an English archaeological expedition in the Middle East discovered the catacombs where King

Solomon's temple originally stood. Catacombs are ancient tunnels dug by hand," Father Langley explained. "It is believed that it was here, under Solomon's temple, that the Grail was originally hidden. However, the British force found that the ancient tunnels had been previously unearthed and raided. The only clue they found was a broken sword. And the sword had a small red cross on its handle.

"While there is more certainty surrounding the crown, many believe the Knights Templar also gained possession of the Grail 800 years before the British discovered the catacombs."

Joel and I sat spellbound by the tale. Jake asked the waiter for a cup of coffee. I wanted a pop, but I didn't want to delay Father Langley's story any more than was absolutely necessary.

"The order of the knights returned to France, but over time, political and religious sentiment shifted. The knights were considered heretics and a threat to the Church," Father Langley said quietly. "Philip IV captured the knight's leader, Jaques de Molay, and subsequently burned him at the stake in, umm..."

"The year 1314," Jake interjected. "If I remember my Money Pit lore properly."

"You do indeed," Father Langley said. "Now I am impressed." So were Joel and I.

Jake knew more, and had more to him, than some mindless dreamer chasing rainbows.

"Anyway," the priest continued, "while de Molay was imprisoned awaiting his sentence, he sent a message to the mysterious order, but the letter was intercepted by forces loyal to the king."

Langley closed his eyes, reciting the ancient inscription from memory. "I am at peace in the arms of Our Saviour. Unto Him I shall be judged as one of many who guard the sacred relics."

"The rest of the Knights Templar evaded Philip's soldiers and fled to Scotland. This was still during the fourteenth century. What happened to the order after that is still a great mystery."

"But what happened to the Crown of Thorns?" Joel pleaded impatiently.

"According to folklore, the order continued as a secret society through the seventeenth century, sworn to protect the spiritual legacies in their possession."

"But how does that tie-in with the Money Pit?" I asked, tossing the remaining, melting ice cubes from my water into my mouth.

"A good question," Jake added "You must admit, Father, there is no hard evidence connecting the knights to the site."

"Well, that is true," Langley admitted. "But there is a great deal of circumstantial evidence. Descendents of the order seem to have disappeared or died out about the same time the pit was dug; there is a record of a large group sailing from Scotland at about this time; and they would certainly have been educated and organized enough to accomplish such an undertaking."

"As would many groups," Jake pointed out.

"True enough," Father Langley conceded.

"While we're on the topic of legends, shall I tell you the one that claims the original works of William Shakespeare are at the bottom of the pit?" Jake asked.

"Really?" I said.

"Some think Sir Francis Bacon actually wrote all the plays, and since none of Shakespeare's original manuscripts exist, it has been surmised that they are buried across the bay," Jake said, pointing in the direction of Oak Island.

"I think your uncle would prefer gold bars to medieval manuscripts," Father Langley said teasingly.

"Father, whatever is down there has great value, financially or historically, and I intend to find out what it is," Jake said. "But all the evidence we've found points to gold."

Father Langley rose to his feet. "I must leave you, as I'm late for a meeting. I will light a candle for your safety," he said kindly. "The good fortune I will leave up to you."

14

A Gathering Storm

JAKE had invited a television news reporter to the island to publicize the cave drawing and stone marker discoveries. He also hoped to satisfy the project's increasingly impatient investors. The reporter and camerawoman arrived in a white sports utility vehicle with *WKRS Television* painted on the side in large red letters. Jake introduced most of the workers to the vehicle's occupants — Rick Lucas and Stephanie Nicholson.

I had been running an errand for Marion when I overheard them unloading their equipment at the far edge of camp. It's not like I was purposely sneaking around, but once you hear two people arguing, it's hard not to tune in. And once they started talking I didn't want them to know I was nearby.

Stephanie was doing most of the work, struggling with a particularly heavy case, while Rick was lazily staring out across the camp.

"Rick!" she yelled, "if you don't help me this second you'll be doing this story alone, and I doubt you'll have much success trying to do the interview and run the camera at the same time."

Rick glared at her for a moment, then reluctantly reached into the car to remove the heaviest of the equipment. "You don't have to freak out on me," he said. "This story's going to put us both on the map — big time!" Rick Lucas didn't fit the stereotype of a reporter. He had a shaved head and a small goatee. He sounded obnoxious. Stephanie Nicholson was older. She must have really wanted to do this story to put up with Rick Lucas for several days.

"So how much do you know about this Morgan guy?" Rick asked coyly.

"I'm not sure there's much to know. He's a fortune hunter from somewhere in British Columbia who believes the Oak Island legend," she said. "The island's the *real* story. Every 30 or 40 years, somebody comes up here convinced there's treasure buried in this hole. They spend a lot of time and money and return empty-handed. It's been going on since the late 1700s. It ought to be fun! People love to hear about this sort of thing. Don't tell me you didn't do your homework on this one? The great Rick Lucas unprepared?"

"Oh, I've done my homework — and then some," Rick said, narrowing his eyes as if scrutinizing something on the horizon, "including an extensive background check on our Mr. Morgan."

Background check? I wondered, as I tried to cling closer to the tree that was providing my cover. I could feel the bark on my cheek as I wondered what they could possibly dig up on my uncle's background.

"I'm not sure I like your tone, Rick," Stephanie said. "This is supposed to be a historical piece — buried treasure, pirates, pieces of eight, yo-ho-ho and a bottle of rum — that sort of thing."

"It's more than that to the people who've invested in this fiasco," he said. "I would imagine they're taking this treasure thing very seriously. Don't you think they'd like to know what's really going on up here?"

"Rick, you stick your nose where it doesn't belong on this piece and you'll lose your job for sure. And no other station will touch you," Stephanie told him harshly. "You've already been responsible for three lawsuits against the station. They don't need a fourth."

"Those weren't my fault! If the station had the guts to back me up..."

"It was slander, Rick! You blew it, okay?" Stephanie said.

"This time I've got the facts to back me up," he smiled. "With the spin I put on this story, news departments from all over the country will line up to offer me a job."

"You're determined to screw this up, aren't you?" Stephanie asked.

"I didn't spend three years in journalism school to cover flower shows and recipes. I plan on getting to the top in this business. This Morgan guy is the chance I've been waiting for," Rick answered.

"Swell," Stephanie said sarcastically. "I can hardly wait."

I felt a sick feeling in my stomach as the pair walked

away. I was constantly amazed at how much trouble adults could stir up.

I told Uncle Jake what I'd overheard.

"Don't worry," he said confidently. "That's just the way some reporters are. Everything will be fine."

But I wasn't so sure.

15

Raise the Treasure!

The shrill alarm shattered the early morning. I bolted upright in my cot, heart racing, immediately wide awake and terrified some terrible accident had occurred. It was 3:15. I heard shouting and yelling. On the tent I could see the shadows of men running. Joel stuck his head inside.

"What's going on?" I shouted above the deafening alarm.

"They've found the chest!" Joel shouted back. "This is it! Hurry up!"

Joel was waiting outside my tent. The area, brightly lit with floodlights, was alive with the shouts of men and the thumping of the diesel generator. We reached the pit as the alarm finally stopped.

The pit's perimeter was roped off with yellow tape. Jake and Marion and two technicians were at the controls of the automatic hoists and the monitoring equipment. Work teams crowded around two television monitors on a table just outside the yellow tape, anxiously watching the scene unfold deep beneath the surface.

Jake watched the action on a laptop computer, communicating with Doug and Orin Jackson, the other crew member below, through a headset. Jake's comments were piped down to them over two speakers. Joel and I could hear and see everything going on — above and below.

The telescoping aluminum support structure was short by about two metres. The chest was slightly deeper down than the historical accounts had led Uncle Jake to believe. Doug and Orin had to dig the two remaining metres by hand in a wide circle to reach the top of the treasure. As a result, they hollowed out a small cavern-like space in which to work, with planks set against the earth walls. It looked dangerous, even from the surface. I wasn't the only one who thought so, for they still wore their safety harnesses in case of trouble.

"Okay, guys," Jake said, his voice echoing throughout the camp. "The Internet feed is up. The world is watching and listening! Doug, why don't you brief us?"

Reporter Rick Lucas leaned in against the tape, positioning himself within speaking distance of Marion. I definitely didn't trust him, remembering the exchange I had overheard the day before.

"Is it safe for them down there?" he asked Marion.

"Barely," she replied, only briefly glancing up from the instruments. "It's gotten very unstable and they're below the protective structure."

"How'd you decide who to send down? I see Morgan's playing it safe," Rick said.

"We drew straws," Marion said, paying little attention to Rick's questions, "including Jake."

"And the losers got stuck doing the digging?" Rick asked.

"No," Marion said, finally turning to face Rick. "The winners! Every member of this crew would like to be down there now." She turned back to the monitors. "Including me."

On the flickering screen, Doug knelt on the floor of the pit in front of a flat black rectangle protruding from the mud. Across its top was a large, heavily corroded chain.

"This is Doug Richfield. I'm 40 metres underground, inside the Money Pit on Oak Island, Nova Scotia. What you see here is the top of a treasure chest buried centuries ago."

"Orin," Jake instructed, "move the camera a bit to the left. That's better. Okay, Doug, go ahead."

"You can just barely make out some of the metal working on the chest's edges and corners, although they're pretty much corroded through. The black discolouration is the result of oxidation combined with the muck down here." Doug made a sour face. "I have to tell you, Jake, this thing stinks! It's rotten!"

Doug carefully probed the lid of the chest with a knife.

"The oak is soft and spongy," he said. "It's surprising it's even held its shape this long."

Excitement and fear made Doug's breath laboured.

"Jake, do you have a good visual of the top of the chest?" Doug asked.

"Orin, to your right," Jake said, studying his monitor. "Your shadow is in the way."

Doug pointed out two fist-sized holes in the top of the waterlogged chest.

"These look like the auger drill holes from the two earlier

expeditions, Jake. The ones from 1849 and 1897," Doug said. "Man, this wood is like oatmeal!"

Marion frantically rushed to Jake's side.

"Jake, tell him not to take the lid off! It'll disintegrate! Tell him they need to use the enclosure pod."

"All right, calm down!" Jake replied, covering the microphone portion of the headset with his hand.

"Jake," Doug called up from below. "We're going to need the *bug jar* down here. This thing's like wet cardboard!"

Jake gave Marion a satisfied look and she returned to her seat.

Rick leaned back against the yellow tape. Stephanie was now at his side, camera at the ready.

"What's the bug jar?" Rick asked Marion.

"That's *their* nickname. The enclosure pod is a bell-shaped capsule," Marion explained. "They'll lower it around the chest and then slide a locking plate beneath it. We can then hoist it up without risking damage to the chest or its contents."

"So why do they call it a bug jar?"

"When you were a kid, did you ever catch bees by trapping them under an upside down jar and sliding a piece of paper under it?" Marion smiled.

"Cute," Rick said sarcastically. I thought it was a perfect explanation. Rick probably never had the curiosity to catch bees. Or more likely he just squashed them.

Two workers connected the cable to the top of the red bell-shaped fibreglass enclosure. It was as tall as a person and 1.75 metres across. It would be a tight squeeze down the final length of the support structure, which was only 2 metres in diameter.

"We're getting the jar ready for you Doug," Jake announced.

"We'll need the pump," Doug answered. "It's still pretty sloppy down here."

"Can you tell where the water's coming from?" Jake asked.

Doug and Orin simultaneously reached down and tasted the watery mud.

"Tastes like chicken," Orin said with a straight face.

"Salty chicken," Doug added. "It's sea water Jake. It's still getting in from the beach somehow!"

"Okay. We'll deal with that later. You two be careful digging out the chest," he advised.

On his hands and knees, Doug slowly and delicately began scooping the muck from around the chest. Orin positioned the mouth of the dredging hose to slurp up the soup-like dirt. Back on the surface, the compressor strained to suck the brackish muck up the length of the 40-metre hose. The dredge coughed and belched as it discharged the slop onto a wire mesh screen. No artifact, no matter how small, would be missed.

The painstaking task of digging the slop away from the fragile walls of the chest continued for 20 minutes. Gradually, centimetre by centimetre, more and more of the chest stood exposed. It stood one-and-a-half metres high, sides bulging like a wet cardboard box filled with rocks.

Doug suddenly stopped digging and looked up with a large smile on his face.

"Jake, I just hit a platform of rotten logs! Ladies and gentlemen, we've reached the bottom of the Money Pit!" Doug said with aplomb.

The crew erupted in cheers and applause as they watched the monitors.

"Ready for the jar!" Doug said.

"Lowering away!" Jake replied. He signalled to Marion and the hoist raised the capsule and then slowly lowered it down the shaft.

Even on the distorted screen, I could see mud oozing through the wood support planks on the sides of the walls. I knew that was a dangerous sign.

"Doug, you might want to check behind you," Jake advised. "Looks like you're getting some seepage."

Doug looked at the mud slowly oozing into the small cavern.

"Can Marion check the lower sensors to see if that's coming from the flood tunnels?" Doug asked from below.

"Already on it," Marion responded. "They're dry. I show no measurable water flow. According to the instrumentation, your goop is working."

"Get the jar into position as soon as it reaches you," Jake urged. "I want you out of there as fast as possible."

Joel and I watched the screen as the bug jar finally reached Doug and Orin. They slid out the base and carefully lowered it over the chest. They rotated it back and forth through the rising muck until it rested firmly on the logs.

Orin and Doug strained to slide the base back through its slot, between the chest and the rotten wood.

"She's in!" Orin said excitedly. "The bug is in the jar!" The workers cheered. So did Joel and I. It was now only a matter of minutes before the long-awaited treasure reached the surface.

Doug and Orin rose from the deep metallic shaft and, momentarily suspended over the mouth of the pit, were loudly cheered by their co-workers. Once on the ground and out of their harnesses, Jake gave them both a congratulatory slap on the back as Doug resumed control of the hoist.

"Raising the jar!" Doug said, easing the controls.

The third winch began turning slowly. As soon as the capsule disappeared from view of the monitor, everyone converged around the pit's perimeter tape. Several anxious minutes passed in which we could only watch the slowly turning gears as it reeled in more and more of the cable. Jake, closest to the pit, saw it first.

"Here she comes!" he called out.

Out of the black depths, for the first time in four centuries, the treasure chest rose from the fabled Money Pit. Feathering the controls, Doug swung the precious cargo over a small platform and lowered it as gently as if handling a baby. The platform groaned under the weight.

Marion and Jake immediately unlocked the base of the capsule. A quick signal to Doug and the top of the bug jar was raised from the long-sought chest. Finally, the legendary treasure! What was considered one of the last great mysteries was about to be revealed.

Stephanie's video camera was all set to capture the climax of the expedition.

"Ugh!" Marion said. "This thing does stink!"

"You'll live," Jake smiled.

Marion handed Jake a hammer and what looked like a large putty knife.

"You do the honours," Marion said.

Jake took the tools and prepared to slice open the side of the soggy chest. Everyone nervously edged forward, holding their collective breath. Jake placed the chisel-like instrument alongside the chest. He gently tapped it with the hammer, slicing through the water-softened wood. The entire side of the chest peeled away as black mud cascaded from the opening. Jake carefully peeled away the other sides of the rotten chest. After countless years buried in darkness the treasure was finally revealed!

16

All That Glitters

"WHAT the heck is that?" Doug asked.

On top of the platform, with the remnants of the sponge-like chest littered around it, was a square-shaped block, roughly the same size as the chest. It was covered with a hard greenish-brown crust. Jake and Marion leaned down to examine the misshapen form.

"It's copper or bronze," Jake concluded. "It's so badly corroded I'm not sure what it is."

"Is it another treasure chest?" Joel asked.

Marion took the hammer and gently broke off a corner piece of the object and studied it carefully.

"Jake," Marion said in a low voice, "this *is* the treasure! These used to be coins! The salt water's destroyed them. Jake, they're worthless!"

Marion's voice was barely above a whisper, but everyone huddled around understood her words. We looked on in silence, stunned by the revelation. For a brief moment Jake sagged, visibly crestfallen, but then quickly recovered. I think he realized everyone was looking to him for strength. Marion continued to chip away at the misshapen block.

"There still might be some coins inside that the salt water didn't reach," Marion said.

"All right," Jake said to the assembled group, "we're going to move this into the portable so we can evaluate what we've got. Let's not jump to any conclusions. Give us an hour to assess this. As soon as *we* know, we'll let all of *you* know."

The way the four men solemnly carried the block through the group of saddened faces reminded me of my grandfather's funeral.

* * *

Two hours passed before Jake, Doug and Marion emerged and rounded everyone up. Jake climbed on top of the small platform. Doug and Marion stood nearby. They didn't look happy.

"All right," Jake began. He looked tired. "This isn't good news. But what I'm about to say doesn't alter the fact that we accomplished something that no one else was able to do — reach the bottom of the Money Pit and finally lay the mystery to rest.

"Originally, the chest was filled with copper and bronze coins. As near as we can tell, when the exploratory drills went through the chest in 1849 and 1897, it allowed sea water to get in. It's had 150 years to decompose and the salt water seems to have seeped into all but a handful of coins in the centre of the chest. All the coins the water reached were either terribly damaged or destroyed altogether.

"I think you all know that gold wouldn't have corroded in sea water. Unfortunately, copper is the most susceptible; and you saw the result. Marion, hand me the sheet," Jake said.

Marion handed him a piece of paper on which they had recorded their findings.

"We were able to identify a number of the coins that weren't destroyed. It looks like a hodge-podge of small denomination coinage from throughout Western Europe — English, French, German, Venetian, Austrian and Spanish. None of the coins we could read were dated later than 1604 AD. So at this point, we'd put the date of the chest's burial in the early 1600s."

"But they must be worth something," a desperate worker asked.

"The few coins that were recognizable and not too badly damaged are probably worth around $15,000," Jake explained. "But that's just an estimate."

"Each?" a worker questioned.

"Total," Marion said sadly.

The group released a collective groan. That final news hit them like a death sentence. They felt betrayed. Some of the most loyal to Jake turned away so others couldn't see the tears in their eyes. Others stared dumbly, as if in shock. After being so close to sharing in a treasure worth millions, they watched their dreams evaporate. It was bitter news to swallow. A few of the men made angry threats about the expedition owing them money. It was painful to watch.

"What the hell kind of treasure is that?" someone called out.

"I don't know the answer to that, Mike," Jake answered wearily. "It doesn't add up. The coins wouldn't have been worth much 400 years ago, so it's unclear why someone went to all the trouble of burying them, digging the flood channels and making the markers. I just don't know."

Rick stood off to the side with Stephanie close by.

"This is sad," Stephanie said quietly, looking at the empty and disillusioned faces. "I feel sorry for them."

"Did you really believe Morgan could pull this off? Wake up Steph! The guy's a loser!" Rick said. "In my mind it's a perfect ending, and I'll add the finishing touches tomorrow."

Marion stepped onto the platform next to Jake to address the group.

"A very real possibility is that the treasure was looted and switched before it ever went into the ground," she suggested to the gathering. "Whether it was pirates, Spanish conquistadors, or whomever, someone may have stolen the actual treasure before it was ever buried. We've seen that in other archeological digs."

"Great," a worker said bitterly, "A 200-year-old wild goose chase!"

"That may very well be the case," Jake admitted. "Doug and I will put together a schedule for breaking camp and getting the equipment back onto the barges. I know all of you want to get back home to your families as soon as possible. I'll talk to each of you a little later. That's all for now guys."

I never understood where Uncle Jake found his spirit.

That morning he sought out each crew member and offered individual thanks for his or her work, effort and sacrifices. He tried his best to put an encouraging spin on a bitterly disappointing situation. It took its toll. By midday he looked haggard and worn. I wondered how much longer he could carry the entire weight of the failed expedition on his shoulders, particularly when he had to be the most broken-hearted person on the island.

17

Bait and Switch

RICK Lucas told Uncle Jake it would be a very informal interview. A few simple questions and answers to be played over the film of the island and treasure. No need to get dressed up. They could re-tape it if it didn't go well. Just a nice, friendly conversation on tape.

Jake, Doug, Joel and I walked toward the main tent where Stephanie and Rick had set up their equipment.

"Jake," Doug said, "You think this is wise?"

"You worry too much, Doug," Jake said. "We came up here to solve a mystery and we did. It wasn't what we hoped to find, but we can't help that. The treasure, the cave drawings, the stone markers, it's all front-page news! Besides, I promised *Insight* an exclusive interview and I won't go back on my word."

I was worried, too. After my accident, I spent a lot of time watching people. For awhile that's all I could do. You can learn a lot about people by paying attention. The things they don't think you see; the position of their feet when they're sitting at a table, what they do with their hands when they're speaking to you, where their eyes wander while you're talking to them; little things. Mostly I could read people's eyes. I could see the whisper-thin difference between someone who hoped you believed them because they told you lies and someone who didn't care if you believed them because they spoke the truth. Some people, like Uncle Jake, had eyes that were sincere and hopeful. But Rick Lucas's eyes were hiding something. I was worried about this interview. I wished I had the courage, or the means, to prevent the whole thing from taking place.

As we entered the tent I noticed a small satellite dish pointing skyward. Inside, two folding chairs were positioned in front of a large camera and a host of blinding lights. Stephanie stood behind the camera. The moment we saw Rick we knew something was up. Gone were his jeans and T-shirt. He wore a pressed white shirt, grey slacks and an immaculate blue blazer. He'd even applied stage make-up. By comparison, Jake looked pale, scraggly and unkempt.

"I smell a rat," Joel said quietly.

"Big time!" I added. I had heard one, and now I smelled one. Joel and I sat in a couple of director's chairs on the other side of the tent.

"Mr. Morgan," Rick said. "I tried to reach you earlier this afternoon. We've had a change of plans. You know how producers can be."

He was being too gracious and too polite.

"They want you for tonight's show, so we'll be doing the transmission live. That's all right isn't it?" Rick said with a big smile.

"Well, I suppose so," Jake obliged.

"Great! We'll do the same thing we talked about," Rick explained. "I'll ask some questions and you just answer them — simple as that!"

Jake calmly took his seat and clipped a small microphone to his shirt. Rick approached Stephanie, fussing with the complex-looking equipment.

"Have you tested the sound levels yet?" he asked.

"What gives? You knew this was going to be live all the time!" Stephanie said in a whisper.

"Shhh!" Rick said. "Watch and learn from the master."

Rick sat down next to Jake, clipping on the other microphone.

"Ready?" he asked Jake.

Jake nodded.

"On my mark," Stephanie said. "Five, four, three, two, one." She pointed to both of them, signifying they were now being broadcast live throughout Canada and the United States.

"The Money Pit of Oak Island has baffled amateur fortune hunters for centuries — until now!" Rick began, sounding every bit the professional reporter. "This is Rick Lucas with *Insight* on location in Nova Scotia, Canada. With me is well-known treasure hunter Jake Morgan who claims to have solved the mystery of the Money Pit."

"Thank you, Rick, it's good to have you here," Jake said, well practised from prior interviews.

"This must have been a bittersweet moment for you, Mr. Morgan. Although you managed to reach the bottom of the hole, it turned out to contain worthless corroded pennies. Isn't that correct?" Rick asked.

"Well, not exactly," Jake said, attempting to correct Rick's opening comment. "Their value certainly isn't what we had hoped for. Unfortunately, the copper and bronze coins, all of which we estimate to be approximately 400 years old, were badly corroded by the salt water. But there's a lot we learned from the expedition."

"Yes, but the treasure itself was certainly disappointing to you, and I would assume to your financial backers?" Rick said.

"Yes." Jake replied cautiously. Now he smelled the rat, too. Joel and I shifted in our chairs. It was like watching an accident unfold in front of your unbelieving eyes, but you're powerless to stop it.

"This must have been an expensive expedition," Rick questioned. "Don't you think with additional research you might have known there was nothing of value down there?"

"Well, no one knew what was in the pit. We made two major discoveries that led us to believe there was a treasure of tremendous value. Those discoveries were cave drawings and stone markers," Jake said.

"Yes, let's talk about this so-called evidence." Rick said. "You claim to have discovered an early cave painting drawn hundreds of years ago depicting the actual burial of the coins?"

"That's correct," Jake answered. "Although it wasn't so much a cave as a small space between..."

"Interesting," Rick interrupted. "Yet I've been told by

historical experts that the natives of this region didn't practise wall painting. Can you explain that?"

"Well, no," Jake answered. "I suppose that adds to its historical significance."

"Don't you think it calls into question its authenticity?" Rick said sharply.

"It's authenticity?" Jake stammered.

"Let's talk about the stone markers," Rick quickly changed the subject to keep Jake off balance. "Cryptic clues chiselled into stone that your group claims to have discovered."

"That's correct," Jake tried to explain. "We were fortunate enough to..."

"Mr. Morgan," Rick said, interrupting Jake, "have the chisel marks been carbon dated?"

"Carbon dating doesn't work on rock, or something that's missing from rock," Jake replied.

"So there's no way to know when the chisel marks were made?" Rick questioned.

"No, unfortunately not," Jake said.

"They could have been made 500 years ago, or 400 years ago?"

"Correct," Jake answered.

"Or even last week?" Rick asked casually.

"What are you driving at?" Jake asked, his temper beginning to rise. Joel and I were tense, and as still as stone.

"Isn't it technically possible that the cave painting and the stone markers could be fabricated to enhance an expedition's reputation with investors? Just technically speaking, of course."

"Both the cave and the markers are genuine," Jake said with finality.

"Of course, of course, but haven't you had problems in the past with your investors?"

Rick was finally getting to his hidden agenda. "I seem to recall allegations on your prior expeditions of inadequate research, poor planning, weak logistics, a host of complaints."

Joel and I looked at one another. This was going downhill fast!

"Every expedition is different," Jake tried to explain calmly. "There are different objectives, different logistics to coordinate. Anyone would tell you that. You can't compare them."

"Yes, but I understand some of your financial backers don't feel you adequately explained the risk. Isn't that true?" Rick pressed on.

"What do you mean?" asked the ambushed Jake.

"Didn't two of your larger investors back out of this project at the last minute?" Rick said, looking at his notes.

"I'm not at liberty to comment on that," Jake said.

"No comment?" Rick repeated, unwilling to accept a non-answer. "You seem to have a pattern of disappointing investors. Isn't that true?"

"Treasure salvage is a high-risk business," Jake said. "We make that very clear to our sponsors."

"Last year you were in Brazil for seven months searching for an ancient city most historians say never existed," Rick said.

"You'll never find it if you're not willing to look for it," Jake responded.

"So let me understand this," Rick said sarcastically, "you spent half a year in a tropical paradise, living on other people's money, searching for something that doesn't exist?"

"That was a legitimate project," Jake said angrily.

"Two years before that, you spent more than one million dollars, again of other people's money, trying to raise the SS *Shonnessy* shipwreck?"

"That's correct," Jake said. "We had located her off the coast of India and came very close to stabilizing her cargo. She went down in 1858, which is well documented. We were hit by a monsoon a month before the season."

"But three investors from that enterprise sued you, didn't they?" Rick said, interrupting Jake again.

"Every one of those lawsuits was thrown out of court as groundless," Jake defended himself.

"But they did file the lawsuits, didn't they?" Rick continued pushing the point.

"Yes, but..." Jake tried to explain.

"Mr. Morgan, have you ever heard the saying *where there's smoke there's fire?*"

Jake didn't answer, but just glared at Rick.

"How do you answer to allegations that you use these expeditions simply as a means as promoting yourself?" Rick asked.

Uncle Jake was struggling to control his anger.

"That's absurd!" he answered.

"But isn't it true that even on this project your crew hasn't been paid? I've been informed by inside sources that you've even had to ration food, as if this was a prisoner of war camp."

"What inside sources?" Jake demanded.

"Mr. Morgan, is it true that there are rumours that you can't account for most of the money you raised for this alleged expedition? Isn't it true there are rumours that you've actually been skimming funds out of this project for your own personal gain?"

Stephanie closed her eyes and rested her forehead against the camera.

"Jeez," she said under her breath. "He just made that one up!"

Uncle Jake's face grew bright red and the muscles in his jaw clamped down. I wanted to jump to his defence but knew better than to try and fight this battle.

Then Uncle Jake stood up, ripped off his microphone and tossed it into Rick's lap. Joel and I leapt out of our chairs, wondering what would happen next.

"No one questions my integrity! This interview's over!" he said.

"You can't just stop in the middle of my interview!" Rick stammered. "The public has a right to hear the truth!"

"That's the last thing they're going to get from you! You've got five minutes…" Jake stopped mid-sentence, realizing that they were still broadcasting.

"Turn that camera off!" he pointed with authority at Stephanie.

"Keep rolling, Stephanie," Rick urged. "This is freedom of the press!"

"Doug," Jake said.

Doug stood up. He only needed to look in Stephanie's direction. The grim look on his face and the tightness in those giant arms spoke for him. Stephanie immediately switched off the camera.

"You've got five minutes to get your gear and vehicle off this site!" Jake commanded.

"You don't own this island!" Rick shouted.

"We have an exclusive and binding lease for 90 days. During that time this is the same as private property, and as of now you're trespassing! Anything not off this campsite will be thrown into the pit!"

"Including smart-ass reporters!" Doug added for good measure.

"Stephanie," Rick backpedaled, "you're a witness! He's physically threatening me!"

"Four minutes!" Jake said looking down at his watch.

Stephanie rushed over between Jake and Rick in an attempt to defuse the situation.

"Mr. Morgan," she began, "obviously this isn't how we wanted all this to turn out. I'm sure that if we all sat down to calmly discuss..."

"Three minutes," Jake said firmly. "You're wasting valuable time!"

"Dammit, Rick!" she cursed as she began gathering up their equipment as fast as she could. Rick watched for a moment, then began scurrying to help.

As the SUV's wheels spun, spraying dirt and gravel behind it, Rick Lucas stuck his head out the window.

"We've already ruined you, Morgan!"

Stephanie drove as fast as possible toward the causeway.

Doug walked up to Jake and slapped him on the shoulder.

"Dang," he said with a grin, "I wish I had your people skills, Jake! You really know how to win friends and influence people."

Jake smiled back thinly.

"That was ugly!" Joel said. I just nodded in agreement.

"I've got a feeling it's going to get even uglier before this is over," Jake said.

18

Hoover's Bones

IT was disheartening to see how quickly people could turn; a little sad to think people were so eager to believe the worst. No one wanted to give Uncle Jake the benefit of the doubt. No one wanted to listen to his side of the story. I guess the more you trust someone, the angrier you get when you think you've been betrayed; and the television interview made a lot of people very, very angry.

Four investors were demanding all their money back and accusing Jake of fraud. A lawyer in Ottawa was trying to organize a class-action lawsuit so *all* of Jake's investors could sue him. Two government agencies wanted to review Jake's financial records and receipts for all his previous expeditions. There were e-mails from eight different newspapers and magazines, informing Jake of stories they were going to print.

Most disappointing, the work crew acted the same way — even Marion. Everyone left the island on the first available barge, which had come to reclaim the bulk of the expedition's equipment. It was as if Jake had something contagious, and the longer anyone stayed on the island, the more likely they'd be infected by the expedition's failure. Doug was the only one who stayed behind, his trust in Jake unshakable. Joel and I stayed close to him, too, eager to demonstrate our confidence in his integrity. But he was so sad we knew our constant presence was hard on him as he had to try to act more optimistic than he was truly feeling. We decided to leave him alone for a while.

Joel and I rode our bikes over the same trail we had ridden a few days earlier. We realized it would be, in all likelihood, our last ride across the island. One final ride before our summer adventure came to an end. It was nice to escape from all the packing and work going on at camp.

Joel waited for me on top of the small rise where the trail forked. The first few times I'd ridden the new bike Joel had been great, riding beside me, taking his time, just to make sure I was okay steering a bike with a prosthetic arm. Now he rode ahead at his own pace, stopping frequently so I could catch up.

"What's up?" I asked, panting just a little and thankful for the bike gears that made going uphill easier. I made it to the top without walking. Every time I did that, I counted it as a victory.

"Look!" he said, pointing to the ramshackle structure. "Someone's there."

A thin wisp of white smoke curled out of a rusted stovepipe chimney. Someone was definitely home.

At that same instant, the cabin's weathered door slowly opened. An old man shuffled out and hobbled down the footpath toward us. He wore a dark grey flannel shirt buttoned tight at the neck, tattered pants held in place by a pair of faded red suspenders, and workboots caked with mud. They were the kind of clothes a logger or lumberjack might wear.

"Morning," he said warmly. "Name's Steiner, Harry Steiner."

"I'm Joel and this is my sister, Emma," Joel volunteered.

"Hi," I said, a little unsure about trusting this unexpected stranger.

"Pleased to meet you," Steiner said. The old man looked at me a second longer than he should have, but it was a much quicker look than most people gave me.

Steiner must have been in his mid-80s. His rough-hewn clothing contrasted with his frail appearance. A ring of uncombed white hair encircled his bald scalp. The top of his head and his angular cheekbones were splattered with age spots. He wore fragile wire-rimmed glasses that couldn't hide the mischievous twinkle in his eyes.

"Aren't you two with that fellah who's digging at the treasure hole?" he asked.

"That's our Uncle Jake," I said proudly, feeling more at ease, for some unknown reason. I leaned my bicycle up against a tree and motioned for Joel to do the same.

"And he found it — the treasure I mean!" Joel bragged, ignoring me.

"You don't say," the old man said flatly. He didn't seem very impressed.

"Well, it wasn't really a treasure; not the usual kind of gold doubloons or jewels," my brother admitted a little sadly. "It was a bunch of copper coins. I guess they're really old, but the salt water ruined them. They're all corroded and stuck together. It's really not much of a treasure at all."

Steiner sat down on a nearby stump so that he was at eye level with us.

"Well I'm sorry to hear that. The important thing is no one was hurt," Steiner said thoughtfully. "Back in the 1960s a Yankee fellah and his family came up here to find treasure. They brought lots of equipment and stayed nearly six months. I'm told they got pretty darn close to it. But then there was some sort of accident. He was killed along with his wife and grandson."

He paused to raise a bony finger at Joel.

"The boy wasn't much older than you," he said menacingly. "There's been a lot of folks who've died over that hole."

Steiner paused a moment, stroking his unkempt hair.

"Besides," he continued, "there's different sorts of treasure. Your uncle should be proud of himself. He's gotten deeper than anybody else who's come here, and there's been a lot of 'em. That's worth something."

"I think he was hoping, well, we were too, hoping it was something really big," I admitted. "After all the stories and legends about it, it was just sort of a letdown."

Steiner stared into space absent-mindedly for a few moments, rubbing the grey stubble on his chin. While he was lost in thought, a tired-looking black Labrador limped painfully down the path. The old dog was white around its muzzle and chest. Steiner reached down and affectionately patted the animal's head.

"That a boy, Hoover," he said.

"Your dog looks hurt," I said. The poor thing could hardly walk.

"What's wrong with him?" Joel asked, finally setting his bike down to get a better look at the old hound.

"I'm afraid there's little that's *not* wrong with old Hoover. He's got arthritis in his shoulders, so he can't walk too well. And those white things in his eyes are cataracts — he's pretty much blind." Steiner told us.

"That's too bad," Joel said sympathetically.

"Well, we all grow old," Steiner smiled. "Me and Hoover been together for as long as I can remember. We're both pretty grey around the snout. But we're good company for each other, aren't we boy?" Steiner stooped down and rubbed his loyal friend under the chin. Hoover closed his milky-white eyes, clearly enjoying his master's affection.

"We both gimp around the island," Steiner said, returning his attention to us, "just taking our own time."

"How does he get around if he can't see anything?" Joel asked.

The old man took his time answering. He had a faraway look in his eyes as he gazed toward the horizon. Then he abruptly looked back to us with a smile.

"Hoover? Hoover gets by on his brains," Steiner grinned. "Smartest dog I've ever seen. Smarter than most folks I reckon."

Joel and I exchanged doubtful looks. Hoover looked like a comfortable companion, but he didn't appear very smart.

"You two look a little doubtful," Steiner observed.

"Well, he's just so old..." I began.

Steiner rubbed the dog's ears.

"Bones. That's how I first knew he was so smart. Bones!" the man said cryptically.

"Bones?" Joel repeated unknowingly.

"Bones. Like any dog, Hoover likes to bury bones. But, of course, he can't see so well, so he can't always find the best places to hide 'em," Steiner said. "Well, now, pretty soon the other dogs figured that out. They'd watch old Hoover bury his bones, and when he'd leave, the other dogs would dig them up and take them. So you know what old Hoover did? He'd bury two bones."

"Two bones?" I repeated.

"He'd bury the big juicy bone deep as he could, and then bury a little small bone on top," the old man proudly explained. "Then when another dog would come sniffing around and start digging, it would find the little bone, stop digging, and happily trot off with the little bone in its mouth. The big bone was still buried. Hoover could come back and retrieve it later."

"That is smart!" Joel admitted.

Steiner's knees creaked and his joints popped as he stood up.

"Well, you two be careful," Steiner said. "It was nice to make your acquaintance."

"Goodbye," we said in unison.

The two old companions hobbled back toward the little shack.

"Yup," Steiner chuckled as he slowly closed the door, "smarter than most people." And with that, the door shut and Steiner and Hoover disappeared inside.

We began to get back on our bikes to complete our cross-island trip. Suddenly, we both froze. We looked at each other the same instant. We both understood!

19

The Auger's Secret

Doug was convinced that the possibility of a second treasure chest was incredibly remote, but would go along with whatever Jake decided. Uncle Jake was looking for any excuse not to quit. Harry Steiner had given him the smallest sliver of hope.

It was Friday morning. The rest of the crew, even Marion, had left the island the night before with the barge of equipment and the chest of corroded coins.

"Even if we find something," Doug told the three of us, "we don't have the manpower or the equipment to bring it up to the surface."

"I'm not leaving this island until we've exhausted every possibility," Jake said. "I'm not ready to give up yet. Not while there's even a slight chance!"

All that morning we worked at setting the drill back up. On the end of the drill was an auger, a sharp metal spiral, half a metre long and nine centimetres in diameter. As the auger bore through the soil, it would capture samples of whatever it passed through. In this way, we could drill a couple of metres, raise the shaft to the surface, analyze the contents, and repeat the process.

Once we had the drill extended to the bottom of the pit, 40 metres below the surface, we were ready. As expected, the first drill sample contained mud. A short settling pipe would keep the mud from filling the drill hole. In the second sample, reaching 40.8 metres, we encountered a bluish-grey clay. Doug told us geological surveys indicated the clay was common in the area, although this was unusually deep for it. We continued drilling.

At 41.5 metres, the auger contained more clay. The same sticky clay clogged the drill at 42 metres. By early afternoon the drill had reached 42.7 metres, three metres lower than the copper coins had been buried. Once again the spiral auger was filled with bluish-grey clay.

"Jake, I think we're kidding ourselves," Doug finally said. "This clay could run down to bedrock. I think it's pointless."

"How many drill lengths do we have left?" Jake asked.

"Enough to get down to 45.7 metres. After that, we're out of equipment."

"Keep drilling!" Jake instructed.

An hour later we raised the auger from 43.9 metres — more clay!

Doug gave Jake a doubtful look.

"Keep drilling," Jake said, but with a lot less conviction.

Jake was beginning to doubt our brief encounter with the old man would lead to anything. I couldn't blame him for that.

Another hour, another .6 of a metre, down to 44.5 metres,

and once again the auger was clogged with the thick clay.

"Jake, it's not a matter of loyalty, you know that. But at some point you have to know when to quit," Doug said. "For your own sake."

Jake hated the idea of quitting, but even he was disillusioned.

"Em, Joel, you two convinced us to try this," he said. "If it was up to me we'd never stop. But Doug's right, I've never had the sense to know when the game is over. What do you two want to do?"

Joel looked to me, deferring to the *wisdom* of his older sister. I looked at the four of us. We were hungry, dirty and extremely tired — both physically and mentally. The more we worked, the more it reinforced the frustration and disappointment of the whole expedition. Doug was probably right — the practical thing, the smart thing, would be to quit and head home.

"One more drill length," I heard myself saying. "Let's give it one more try!"

Joel nodded his approval to me.

"You heard the boss," Jake said to Doug. "No giving up yet."

"I can see I'm outnumbered," Doug shook his head good-naturedly. "There's no doubt you three are related!"

Shortly thereafter we raised the auger and shaft that had reached 45 metres. Doug anxiously laid it on the table.

"Clay!" he said dejectedly, "more damn clay. I'm sorry, Jake."

I took a chunk of the clay from the bottom of the screw-shaped drill. It had a rough, sandy texture as I squeezed it between my fingers. But there was something else mixed in with the clay; some sort of brown strings.

"What's this stuff?" I asked. "Roots?"

"Not down that far," Doug answered. "Let me see what you've got."

He took the clump from me and examined it closely.

"Jake!" he looked up in astonishment. "It's coconut fibres!"

Jake rushed over and meticulously studied the fibres.

"You're right," he said, "just like in the flood trenches. And there's only one way this could have gotten down that far. It was purposely buried."

"I'll get the last drill extension," Doug said with renewed energy. We forgot how tired and hungry we were as we prepared the final length of the drill.

We slowly withdrew the last and final auger length, which had reached 45.7 metres.

The first 55 centimetres was a tangle of brown coconut-husk fibres. The lowest 18 centimetres contained a thin layer of a wax-like substance followed by 12 centimetres of dry, crumbly wood. The auger was empty after that.

We all came to the same conclusion. We had drilled through the top of a second treasure chest! Old Harry Steiner had been right. Even though the top of the chest was fragile with dry rot, the most important fact was that it was dry. The six metres of clay had acted like a giant cork. Whatever was buried 400 years ago had been completely protected from the sea water. But how would we bring the treasure to the surface? We had no food left, let alone the right equipment, we had no money, and we were running out of time.

20

Missing Ashes

UNCLE Jake's mood changed with the discovery of a second chest six metres below the original cache of damaged coins. He felt particularly grateful to Harry Steiner.

"Let's invite your friend Harry over," Jake suggested. "He may have saved the day for us. I'd like to thank him in person."

"We'll go and invite him," I volunteered. I got the funniest feeling from that old man. Distrust had turned into genuine affection, and yet the whole thing was sort of odd. "I think he'd like that. He seemed a little lonely. Can his dog come, too?"

"Absolutely!" Jake said, smiling.

"Can you can show him what we've found so far and explain everything to him?" Joel asked.

"Well, I'll explain what I can," Jake said. "His name still rings a bell but I can't seem to place it. Anyway, it sounds like his memory is better than mine. He'll probably remember if our paths have ever crossed."

"We'll be right back," Joel said, picking up a bike helmet and tossing the other to me.

"Okay. Be careful," Jake said encouragingly. "I'll be ready for company."

I felt more confident with each ride. I still wasn't able to keep up with Joel, and came to realize that maybe I never would, but it was fun to feel the wind in my face and a sense of freedom.

We stopped near the small shack, leaned our bikes against a tree, and walked up the overgrown path to the weather-beaten shack. Joel knocked loudly on the door.

"Hello!" he called out. "It's Joel and Emma from the dig."

There was no answer.

"Maybe he's outside," I suggested. I could feel the little hairs go up on the back of my neck.

"Hello!" Joel called louder, turning the doorknob.

"Joel! You can't just walk into somebody's house!" I said.

As usual, he ignored me. The door swung open easily. We were immediately confronted by a disagreeable stench of mildew and musty air.

"It stinks in there," I said from behind Joel, covering my nose.

"Wait until you see the inside," he warned me. "It's a dump!"

Nettles and blackberry vines grew in front of the broken windowpanes, making the cabin dark. The floor was littered with debris — broken chairs, rusty beer cans, shards of broken windows, and the soiled cotton stuffing from a ripped-up mattress. Everything appeared a dull grey from a thick layer of dust.

"Check out the ceiling," I said nervously, pointing up. "It doesn't look very safe!"

In fact the whole cabin was creepy and made me nervous. The ceiling sagged dangerously. Years of accumulated moss and windfall on the roof outside bowed the rotting timbers above us.

"Em, I don't think anybody's been in here for years," Joel observed.

"Even the spiders have given up on this place," I said. "It gives me the creeps. Let's go!"

"Let's look around first and make sure we're not missing something," Joel said, looking around the disheveled surroundings. Our search yielded little. Anything of value or offering information was long gone. Joel spotted a folded piece of yellow paper, just barely visible under the leg of a dirt-covered table.

"This might be something," he said, removing the paper from beneath the table leg. "Maybe it's a message, or a map!"

I wiggled the tabletop and it wobbled noticeably on its uneven legs.

"I think it's just there to steady the table," I told him.

"I think you're right," he said, a bit disappointed. He unfolded what looked to be a bit of old newspaper.

"President Johnson commits military advisors to Southeast Asia," he said, reading the headline.

"Whoa! That's old," I said, definitely feeling uncomfortable being there. I tried to stick as close to Joel as possible, while keeping a sharp eye out for any spiders that might consider landing on me.

"There's an address label on the edge," Joel said. He tilted the paper back and forth in the dim light. "H. Steiner, 915 Mueler Lane, Rochester, New York. Well, this is his place all right. He must have brought this with him."

Joel's eyes widened suddenly.

"Wait a minute, Em," Joel said. He withdrew the tightly folded message from his pocket that he found our first night on the island. He unfolded it and compared it to the newspaper from under the table leg.

"Take a look," he said. The small message perfectly matched a missing corner torn from the old newspaper's front page.

"So it was Steiner," I said, looking at the papers in Joel's hands.

"It must have been," Joel said.

"He must have known about the second chest all the time," I said.

"I wonder if he knows what's in it?" Joel wondered aloud.

"No one knows," I said. "But Uncle Jake's definitely going to want to talk to Mr. Steiner next time we see him."

I carefully picked my way across the junk-strewn floor to examine the small pot-bellied stove. I opened the black metal door and looked inside. This is where the cabin really started to get confusing.

"The stove hasn't been used either," I said.

"Em, I know I saw smoke the other day," Joel said.

"I thought so too, but there aren't any ashes in here —

none at all!" It looked like it had been cleaned out a long time ago. It didn't make sense. It was like the day I felt we were being watched in the woods — a feeling without any real evidence.

"He must live somewhere else," Joel suggested. "You know, like this is his old place."

"I guess so," I said. Neither of us knew what else it could be.

"Let's go back to camp. This place is beginning to make my clothes stink," I said.

We walked outside to our bikes, shutting the door behind us.

"Jake's going to be disappointed. He really wanted to thank him," Joel said. "But we'll probably run into him again."

"I suppose so," I said, but I didn't really think we would.

Joel and I didn't talk much about Harry Steiner after that. The inside of his cabin didn't make any sense. But it wasn't the last we'd hear of him.

After our unsuccessful trip to find Steiner, Joel and I concentrated on two jobs. First, we made a detailed list for Doug of all the equipment left behind on the island — everything from oxygen cylinders to individual tools. Secondly, Jake asked us to scrounge together dinner for the four of us. All we found were two-dozen berry-flavoured nutrition bars and three large boxes of raisins.

Jake and Doug "worked the phones" as they called it. Doug concentrated on the equipment — what we needed, or actually what we could get by with, for a last-ditch attempt to unearth the second chest. He called every equipment manufacturer, distributor and dealer in the area, frantically trying to catch them before they closed for the weekend. Jake had the tougher job. He was desperately trying to raise enough money to obtain whatever equipment Doug could track down.

It was 9:30 p.m. when we finally gathered for our last project status meeting and eat our meager dinner. The setting sun ringed the hills across Mahone Bay with a golden orange halo.

When we brought Jake and Doug their nutrition bar and raisin dinner, neither looked very optimistic.

"You two get enough to eat?" Jake asked.

"Sure," I said. I was actually still hungry, but this was no time for complaining.

"I had four bars," Joel said.

"Okay," Jake said wearily. "I don't want you two to go hungry. Doug, let's go over this from top to bottom. Why don't you start?"

"All right," Doug said. "Basically, we're running out of time. The pressure seems to be increasing down there. The 40-metre level where the first chest was is slowly refilling with mud. If the water's coming in from the beach, we'll have a major problem in three days; it's one of the highest tides of the year — more than four metres. The thing is, I don't have any answers as to why the water is getting in. The goop shouldn't be breaking down yet. It should last six months before dissolving."

"We've got another time problem — a new one," Jake said. "The government called. Seems we've become undesirables since that TV show. Our work permits are being cancelled, effective Wednesday. They made it very clear they were prepared to use force if necessary to escort us from the island."

"Wednesday! That's only five days," Doug blurted. "They've got to be kidding!"

"That only gives us four days to work," Joel observed.

"Correct," Jake said. "I spoke with our lawyer. To get back here with an exclusive on the property we'd be tied up in court for years with dozens of government agencies."

"All our work wasted?" I asked. This couldn't be happening.

"More likely someone else will dance in here and take advantage of everything we've done," Doug said angrily.

"What's the equipment status?" Jake asked Doug.

"Well, I've got good news and bad news," he said. "Which do you want first?"

"I could use a little good news," Jake said. "Let's start with that."

"The only things we still have fully operational are the sensors, computers, communication gear and the small drill system. Aside from that, we're pretty much starting from scratch.

"Most importantly, we need some sort of support system as we go deeper, particularly if the water continues to be an issue. We'll need a flap-valve dredge pump that can pull 1,000 litres per minute up a 50-metre hose. I'd prefer a *Rupp*, but…"

"Doug," Jake interrupted, "give me the bottom line here. Have you located what we need and what it will cost?"

"I found a used equipment place in Chester that has enough of what we need to get by. They're the only ones who could get the stuff here on such short notice," Doug explained. "But, Jake, I've got to be honest with you. Even if we get the stuff it'll be sketchy. The stuff is used; some of it dating back to the 1960s, and sounds pretty unreliable. That being said, with some luck, we could get by with it."

"That was the *good* news?" Jake asked. "What's the bad?"

"The price," Doug answered. "I spoke directly with Dorsey, who owns the company. For some reason this guy has a real attitude about us. No rentals, everything must be purchased; and no credit, cash only. I got the impression he doesn't care if he sells it to us or not! Definitely a weird guy."

"How much are we talking about for everything?" Jake asked.

"All in, just north of $22,000."

"Any chance for negotiation?" Jake questioned.

"I doubt it," Doug said. "He knows he's the only supplier that has what we need. How did you do on the money side?"

"I'm afraid that's in the bad news category," Jake confessed. "I made more than 70 calls to sponsors we've worked with in the past. The ones who actually returned my calls don't want anything to do with this. Doug, have we considered all the possible ways to reach the treasure?"

"Couldn't we just lower a dredge hose down the drill hole and suck out the treasure?" I suggested.

"Theoretically, that's a good idea, Emma," Doug said. "I even considered that myself. There are too many problems. The hose could collapse from pressure. If the treasure is too heavy it won't work; if it's fragile it will be destroyed. And, of course, we need a pump, and they're not cheap. Plus, if someone wasn't down there to position the hose properly, we might wind up trying to drain the Atlantic Ocean."

"How about shovels?" Joel asked.

"Suicide," Doug quickly said. "I'm convinced the pit will cave in without support and we'd still need to get fresh air down there."

"So where does that leave us?" I asked.

"Guys, I've racked my brains on this," Jake said. "I just don't see a solution. Doug?"

"Me neither," Doug said quietly. "We need the equipment."

21

Blood and Water

IT was nearly midnight, East Coast time, when I called home. I had to tell Mom and Dad that we were coming home. Mostly, I hoped they hadn't seen the television interview, especially Dad. The phone rang seven times before it was finally answered. I thought I had been disconnected when there was a clicking sound right after Mom's familiar "Hello?"

"Hello, are you still there? It's Emma."

It wasn't a very good connection and it was hard to hear.

"Oh, Em, I'm glad you called! I'm just clearing up the kitchen. We had a late supper. How's your, I mean, how are you doing?" Mom asked with concern.

"I'm fine."

"And Joel?" she asked.

"Joel is acting like Joel," I said.

"Good!"

"I was calling to see if you or Dad had been watching TV lately."

"Em, it's been terrible here since that TV show!"

"You saw it then," I said. I was disappointed, but not surprised.

"Everyone in town either saw it or heard about it. And the local station has played it over and over. They even put the interview on the radio! The *Register* has run several stories; all of them negative," Mom explained. "We've had so many calls from reporters, and Jake's old investors, we haven't been answering the phone. For some reason I thought this might be you calling."

"What did Dad say?" I asked nervously.

"We were watching television together when the interview was first on. His face just got redder and redder. He didn't say a word. He refuses to discuss it. I've never seen him so mad."

"You should have been here," I said. "That guy from the show was a total snake! Jake had to throw him off the property!"

"How is Jake holding up through all this?" she asked.

I was glad someone was concerned about Uncle Jake, who really was the one suffering from all of this.

"He's pretty discouraged right now, although you know he never tries to show it."

"Oh, I know it," Mom agreed.

"I told you about the first treasure last time we talked, didn't I?"

"First?" Mom said. "Is there another?"

I told Mom about our discovery of the second chest and for the first time I told her about Jake's money problems.

"Everybody thinks he's a crook because of that interview," I said.

"It didn't look good," Mom agreed.

"So he can't raise more money to get the real treasure, and everyone's threatening to sue him! It's a mess. I'm not supposed to know this, and please don't tell Dad," I whispered into the phone, "but Jake's sold everything he had just to get this far. A few days ago he even sold his airline ticket to get home! I think he's pretty much broke."

"Poor Jake!" Mom said sympathetically.

"Anyway, the expedition is over," I said. "I'm not sure exactly what time our flight lands in Vancouver, but we fly out of Halifax tomorrow late afternoon."

"All right," she said. "Just let us know when you find out your flight times and we'll pick you up."

"Okay."

"Give my love to Joel," she said.

"Say hi to Dad," I said.

"Love you, Em."

"Love you, Mom," I said, hanging up.

As I was hanging up, I distinctly heard a second phone disconnecting at home; the sound you hear when someone else has been listening to your conversation on another phone line.

It was afternoon by the time Joel and I were finally ready with our bags packed. Joel had lost his Air Canada ticket, and it took us an hour to find it. Jake loaded our suitcases into the Jeep.

"Tell your folks I'm not sure when I'll get back to town," Jake said. "It'll take awhile to clean up all the loose ends from this."

Doug came running out of the portable lab, paper in

hand. He was in such a hurry he nearly stumbled.

"Jake!" he said breathlessly. "I just printed this e-mail. I think you'd better read it!"

"Who else wants a piece of my hide?" Jake said tiredly. "I haven't got anything left for anybody to take. Just put it in the file with the rest of them."

"I think you had better read this one," Doug said, handing Jake the piece of paper, "Aloud!"

"Okay," Jake agreed. "To Doug.Richfield@Tsite.com; transmitted 1:20 p.m. Eastern Daylight Time…"

"Just the letter," Doug said.

"This is to serve as notification that $22,415 has been wired into account #53W461-01 at the Chester branch of the Royal Bank of Canada for the benefit of Jake L. Morgan. Funds are available for immediate disbursement."

Jake looked up in amazement.

"Look down to the bottom," Doug instructed.

"Source of funds: Pacific Coast Savings of Brackendale, BC, from the account of John M. Morgan."

Within a few minutes Jake was on the phone with Dad.

"John, this means more to me than you can imagine," Jake said, his voice thick with emotion. "But I can't take this from you. You can't afford to lose this! It's too much!"

"Jake, I've had to watch that damn interview every time I turn on the TV. I've had to read about it in the paper. I've had to listen to everybody in town gossiping about it. And now we're being hounded by the press for interviews," Dad said. "I'm sick and tired of everybody taking cheap shots at my little brother! Take the money — that's an order!"

"Thanks, John," Jake said.

"One more thing," Dad added.

"Yes?" Jake asked.

"Find the treasure, Jake!" Dad said with surprising determination. "Show them what Morgans are made of!"

I'd read that "blood was thicker than water," but always wondered if it applied to our family. That day I got my answer. I'd never been prouder of my Dad.

22

Voices from the Past

WE entered the small café in Chester, greeted by the usual stares of the townspeople. Jake was somewhat of a celebrity now, although not a very well-liked one. I, of course, provided an additional attraction for gawking. I used to play a game with myself. I'd see how long someone would stare at me. I thought certain types of people would stare longer than others, but I gave it up. They all stared longer than I liked.

Now, almost seven months after the accident, I no longer cared. I made up my mind that I wouldn't let it bother me.

Jake approached a short, stocky man with curly hair and thick arms standing behind the counter.

"I'm looking for Ron Dorsey," Jake explained. "I was told I could find him here."

"I'm Ron Dorsey," the man answered. "What is it that you want?"

"There must be some mistake," Jake said. "I was told you ran a heavy equipment business."

"I do. I also own this café," Dorsey explained. "On Sundays the equipment business is closed and I work here."

"Well," Jake said, watching Joel and I climb onto the old-fashioned counter stools. "Why don't we start with two of your largest cinnamon rolls, two milks and a cup of coffee for me — with cream."

"Coming right up," Dorsey said. Joel and I watched hungrily as Dorsey cut two huge cinnamon rolls, and brought over two tall glasses of cold milk. Once that was done, Jake returned to the real reason for our visit.

"I'd like to talk to you about buying some equipment," Jake said. "Eleven metres of one-metre drainage pipe, a four-metre Haxton Crane, six-metre if you got it, and..."

"Look, Mr. Morgan, we all know who you are. We seen you on the news," Dorsey interrupted. "But if you're looking for help in this town..."

"I don't follow," Jake replied. I could see Uncle Jake was confused by Dorsey's cold treatment.

"I guess you don't quite understand what you've done," he said curtly. "We used to get a lot of tourists here to see the Money Pit. There was always lots of speculation and stories about what was down there. We had people coming from all over. Now you go and solve the puzzle. No more mystery, no more tourists, no more business."

"That's not his fault," I said defensively.

"That's all right, Em," Jake said. He held up his hand to signal the conversation might go better without my involvement.

"It may be all right for you, but a lot of folks up here make their living on tourism," Dorsey said. "And what do you pull out of the hole? A bunch of crud from what I've heard. Nope, we'd all be better off if you'd never found anything."

"But that's why we're still here. It's not over," Jake said. "There's another chest farther down. We're here to get supplies to make one final push. And this might be a treasure that would draw tourists from all over the world."

"What makes you think there's a second treasure?" Dorsey asked skeptically, "or that it won't be more of the same crud?"

"There's a second chest and the water hasn't gotten to it. Whatever's down there is perfectly preserved," Jake explained. "Under those conditions, even copper coins could be worth a fortune to a museum or collectors."

"Sounds to me like you just don't know when to quit." Dorsey didn't mean it as a compliment.

"Morgans never quit," Joel said.

"These two convinced me to go deeper," Jake said proudly, putting his arms around Joel's and my shoulders.

"The kids?" Dorsey asked.

"We got the idea from the old man living on the island," Joel said defiantly. "His dog actually gave us the idea."

"There's no old man on the island," Dorsey said.

"Yes, but..." Joel started to explain.

"Listen, Morgan," Dorsey interrupted Joel. "I'd like the stories to be true as much as the next guy, but you're not giving me much to go on. You can't expect people to believe you because of somebody's dog."

A red-headed waitress working the tables out front walked behind the counter.

"What's all the fuss about?" she asked her boss.

"They claim there's another treasure farther down in the pit," Dorsey said, gesturing toward Jake.

"No kidding?" the waitress said, snapping her chewing gum. "How do you figure that?"

"Their dog told them," Dorsey answered sarcastically.

"Not *our* dog," Joel corrected him. "Harry Steiner's dog."

Dorsey and the waitress jerked to attention. Joel had hit a nerve.

"Whose dog did you say?" the waitress asked slowly.

"Harry Steiner's." This time I answered. "We met him by his old cabin. It's more of a shack really."

The two exchanged nervous glances.

"That's not funny," the waitress said sternly. She acted like Joel and I had done something wrong.

"Doris, go back to the storeroom and get that black scrapbook near the freezer," Dorsey ordered. He turned his attention to Joel and me. "So you'd recognize him again if you saw his photo?"

"I suppose so," I answered for both of us. "We only spoke to him for five minutes."

The gum-snapping waitress returned with an oversized scrapbook bulging with photos, newspaper articles, napkins, letters and other memorabilia.

Dorsey took the scrapbook and leafed through it intently, one page at a time. He stopped on a page with a faded newspaper clipping with a large black-and-white photograph. Dorsey swung the book around. Both the newspaper and the

Scotch-tape holding it in place were faded yellow.

"That your man?" Dorsey asked us, pointing.

"That's him all right," Joel said. "He looks exactly the same!"

"That's definitely him," I said with conviction. "But it's not a very good picture."

Uncle Jake leaned over to get a look.

"Looks like a friendly sort," Jake said, sipping his coffee. "I wish he'd been around the other night..." The cup slipped from Jake's trembling hand, nearly spilling on the carefully preserved scrapbook.

"Damn!" Jake said uncharacteristically. He rarely swore in front of us. "Now I remember the name — Harold L. Steiner from New York!"

"What?" I asked. "Who is he?"

"Steiner came up here in 1964 to dig up the treasure," Dorsey explained.

"But the support scaffolding collapsed while he and his family were standing on it," Jake continued in a subdued voice.

"You see," Dorsey said, looking directly into Joel's and my eyes, "Harold Steiner's been dead for nearly 40 years."

Uncle Jake was the most shaken. He knew all the legends surrounding the Money Pit. There were stories of nearby residents, who as children claimed to have seen ancient men, shrouded by mist, digging in the dead of night. There were tales that the treasure would remain a secret until the last oak tree on the island was gone. Perhaps the most unsettling to us was the belief that the treasure couldn't be discovered until one more person died trying to recover it. Six treasure hunters had already perished over the years.

Jake had always dismissed the legends as the silly ramblings of superstitious country folk. Yet he knew Joel and I wouldn't lie about meeting Harry Steiner. Jake also realized Steiner was the sole reason we'd continued digging. I think he was desperately searching for a rational, logical, scientific explanation. But he couldn't come up with one; nor could Joel and I explain it.

Ron Dorsey was at a loss, too. Yet rather than kicking us out or calling us a bunch of liars, he just looked straight at Joel and me for the longest time. Finally he looked back at Jake. "Okay, tell me what equipment you need."

The chilly ocean wind blew hard as we walked back through the small coastal town. The streets were mostly deserted, it being a cold Sunday morning. We passed the small stone church. Around its perimeter were tall old-fashioned lampposts adorned with square yellow banners. The banners each had a large crucifix on them. There were probably 15 or 16 of them, and they gave the grey chapel a colourful, festive air.

One of the banners had broken free from one of its two fasteners, and hung sideways. As we walked beneath it, we were too busy listening to Uncle Jake explain the equipment to notice that the crooked banner's crucifix now had a strong resemblance to a large "X."

23

Beyond Our Grasp

THE equipment was delivered to the island later that day. It was 30 years out of date, beaten, battered and left over from a once-thriving logging industry. Most of it was dangerously unreliable. But we had no choice. We had run out of time. Jake had to settle for whatever equipment was close at hand.

The only protection against a cave-in for the last 8 metres would be a thin, heavily dented, drainage pipe less than a metre in diameter. It would be a very tight squeeze for anyone trying to get through. It looked frail and weak compared to the thick aluminum support that framed the pit's upper portion.

Doug's biggest concern was the hoist system. It was based on an antiquated and poorly maintained hydraulic system. Worn fluid hoses ran alongside the master controls at the rear of a protective steel hood.

"The whole system stinks!" Doug said over and over.

Despite Doug's constant cursing and worrying, we cobbled together an ingenious device to try and reach the treasure — a 1.5-metre drill head fastened to a portable motor, attached to one end of the 8-metre drainpipe. In a vertical position, the pipe could burrow straight down. The dredging hose was lowered inside the pipe, so as the drill bore through the clay and muck, the pump could suck it up to the surface. We lined the outside and inside of the pipe with sensors, so pressure and water flow could be tracked.

Because of the danger and poor equipment, Jake insisted he should shoulder the risk of going into the pit. Doug was probably too big to squeeze through the drainpipe, anyway.

Jake hovered on a line at 36 metres. By leaning against the metal walls he could steady the length of pipe as it drilled toward the second chest.

"Ready to go," Doug signalled to Jake.

Doug and Jake communicated through their headsets.

"Both pumps working?" Jake asked.

"The dredge is at 90 percent capacity, and the oxygen line is in the green," Doug said. "Cross your fingers!"

"Once the motor starts I won't be able to hear anything," Jake explained. "Make sure you stop the drill at 45.5 metres. It'll tear the chest apart if it goes too deep."

"Got it boss. Ready?"

"Ready!" Jake replied, putting his earplugs in. Jake started the motor, setting the sharp teeth of the drill head in motion.

"Easing the tension," Doug said to us.

As Doug slowly let out the cable supporting the long pipe and heavy drill, the pipe began to inch its way into the ground.

"I'm showing the drill head at 40.5 metres," Doug announced. "I think this crazy thing's going to work!"

Far below, Jake strained to keep the pipe positioned straight up and down in the direction of the second treasure chest.

"Forty-one point eight metres!" Doug called out. "It's working! We're going to make it!"

The dredge pump spat out the watery clay. We should have noticed something wasn't adding up. The clay from the auger drill had been thick and dry. This sludge was wet. Water was still seeping in from somewhere.

"Forty-three point nine metres," Doug announced. "We're almost there! Forty-four point five, 44.8, slowing down, slowing down, 45.1, and 45.4! Stopping the hoist!"

Jake stopped the drill's motor and repositioned his headset. The top of the drainpipe and the bottom of the aluminum support structure overlapped by about a third of a metre.

"Where are we?" Jake asked.

"The end of the pipe should be right at 45.5 metres," Doug said.

We lowered Jake through the narrow pipe to disconnect the motor and drill head. After hoisting Jake out of the way, Doug was able to pull the motor back to the surface. The only thing now standing between Jake and the treasure chest was an 8-metre length of narrow dark pipe.

"Okay, Doug, take me down for a look!" Jake said hopefully. "Lower me to 45 metres."

Doug carefully worked the controls to slowly lower Jake to within a couple of metres of where the treasure should have been.

"Doug!" Jake called up on the microphone. "There's water down here!"

"I'm reading some flow on the outside of the pipe," Doug explained. "Jake, the pressure readings are off the chart! It doesn't look good!"

"Damn! I can't quite reach it!" Jake said in frustration. "It must be just beneath the water!

Over the loudspeaker, we could hear the pipe groaning under the pressure.

"Jake, you hear that?" Doug exclaimed. "I'm not kidding about the pressure build-up. I'm not sure how much longer the thin pipe will hold!"

"Doug, I can feel the chest with my foot! It's just a bit below the water level."

We froze as we heard a loud grating sound.

"Jake!" Doug shouted. "You're coming out now! The sensor readings are going nuts!" He slowly engaged the hoist's gearing to raise Jake back out the narrow pipe.

"Pull me out so I can go back down head first!" Jake pleaded. "I'll be able to get my hands on it!"

The expression on Doug's face made it clear that he didn't like the idea of Jake going back down into the thin pipe. Joel and I were worried, too.

"Okay," Doug said to himself. "He's almost to the support structure."

Suddenly there was a loud crash and the whole campsite seemed to shudder. At the same instant, Jake cried out in pain through the headset. The hoist stalled. Doug quickly shifted it into neutral.

"Jake! What happened? Are you okay?"

"The top part of the drain pipe's collapsed!" Jake groaned. "It caught my leg, just below the knee. I can't budge it."

Joel and I exchanged a frightened look.

"How bad is your leg?" Doug asked, maintaining his composure.

"It hurts, but I don't see any blood. I'm pinned down here, Doug!"

"Tell me about the pipe," Doug asked.

"Okay," Jake said, his voice becoming more calm. "It's crushed to about 15 centimetres at the widest part, less than that where it's got my leg."

"What will we do?" Joel asked in a frightened voice.

"Quiet!" Doug snapped. "Give me a minute here, Jake."

"I'm not going anywhere, friend," he replied.

Joel and I looked hopefully toward Doug, who gazed intently at the controls.

"Okay," Doug finally said. "Hang on, Jake, I've got an idea. Em, Joel, run to the Jeep and bring me the grey toolbox in the back. Hurry!"

We ran to the Jeep and raced back with the heavy metal box.

Minutes later Joel was lowering a line to Jake.

"We're lowering a present down to you," Doug said.

"What?"

"It's the jack from the Jeep. Try to wedge it between the sides of the pipe. Then lever it like you're changing a tire. It ought to open the pipe enough so you can get out."

"Doug, you're brilliant!" Jake said.

I couldn't have agreed more. I could see why Jake had insisted that Doug work on all his salvage projects.

"Okay, I'm free!"

The three of us cheered.

"I'm all right, but my leg's pretty sore," Jake said into his microphone. "Doug, there's too much pressure. I put everything I had into that jack, but the opening is less than 30 centimetres wide. We can't even lower the camera through it. If we try and remove the jack it'll be crushed flat."

"I'm sorry, Jake, but if that's the case, you need to get out of there. The rest of the thing could collapse at any minute," Doug called down.

"I know," Jake said dejectedly.

"Are you ready?" Doug asked.

Jake sadly shined his headlamp down the long, narrow pipe. The dim beam of light reflected off the brown water far below. He had come within less than a metre of realizing his dream; he had even touched it with his outstretched foot. Now it seemed permanently out of reach.

"Jake! Do you hear me?" Doug asked.

"Yes," Jake replied. His voice sounded unusually distant and tired. "Pull me out. The game's over. We can't get it."

On the surface, Jake was quiet and subdued. His leg was bruised and swollen.

"Jake, for what it's worth, I doubt we could have gotten it anyway," Doug said. "The water down there is gaining on us. Best case, we would have had a 30-minute window to get it early tomorrow when the tide is just right. There's too much pressure on that cheap pipe. Once the water reaches high tide, that whole thing could collapse."

"Thanks," Jake answered quietly. He limped to the portable lab and slowly closed the door behind him.

24

Fallen Stars

JOEL and I walked toward Jake and Doug's campfire. The sky was a twinkling canopy of lights. Here on the edge of North America, no fluorescent lights dimmed the heavens and the faintest star glimmered brightly.

I once read that we were actually gazing up through history. Stars were so distant that the light we saw took hundreds, even thousands, of years to reach us on earth. Some of the stars we saw may actually have burnt out and vanished ages ago. Somewhere above, in that timeless panorama, were stars whose brilliance first began their earthbound journey centuries ago, at the exact moment a group of men, shrouded in secrecy, first set foot on Oak Island. It was as if the answer to the mystery was all around us, but impossible to grasp.

Uncle Jake and Doug were discussing the final details of the expedition as Joel and I approached.

"The truck should get here by noon," Doug said. "We'll be able to get everything loaded before dark. Dorsey said he'd give us a partial refund. He said he was sorry it didn't work out." Doug took a long drink from a half-empty beer bottle, emptying it. There were two empty bottles by his feet.

"We're all sorry about that," Jake said, staring into the fire.

"Jake, if it wasn't for the tide we'd have a shot. We could get the right support structure in place, pump the sucker out, drill down and pluck it out," Doug said, as much to himself as to Jake. "By 5:30 a.m. tomorrow, at high tide, we're sure to lose that lower section. Then it'll gradually start refilling, probably even separating some of the larger pieces."

"It can't be helped, Doug," Jake said dejectedly. "Things just didn't work out."

Doug rose to his feet.

"Well, I'm going to turn in," he said, as Joel and I sat down. "You kids get some sleep tonight. We've got a long day tomorrow breaking camp." We nodded.

"We'll get 'em next time boss," Doug said with false optimism.

"This is the fourth dry hole in a row, Doug," Jake said, still looking into the fire. "Do you really think there will be a next time?"

Doug looked down at the empty bottle in his hand.

"I suppose not," he said sadly. "Listen, Jake, no matter what the press, or the investors, or anybody says, you're first class. I wouldn't have stuck it out with you if I didn't think so. I don't regret any of it."

"Thanks, Doug," Jake said, looking up from the fire with a weak smile.

"See you in the morning," Doug said, slowly walking back to his tent.

The three of us didn't speak for several minutes. Each of

us stared into the fire, lost in our own private thoughts.

"What now?" I finally asked.

"Now? Tomorrow we head out. You heard Doug. We've just plain run out of time," Jake answered quietly. "You two have been a great help. We couldn't have gotten nearly so far if it hadn't been for the both of you. I'm very proud of you. I'm sorry we couldn't get the second treasure chest, but things don't always work out the way you hope they will."

"And that would have made you rich," Joel said sympathetically.

"Oh, I suppose so, Joel. But it's funny; it really wasn't about the money. In the past, I've gone after treasure to become rich," Jake said, stirring the dying fire with a stick. "But this time it was different. I just wanted to solve the mystery. That was all. No one knows what's buried down there. They've been trying for 200 years to find out. It's a puzzle no one can solve. That's what I really wanted. I wanted to be the one who solved the mystery of Oak Island."

"Like the first person to climb Mount Everest or something," I said.

"Something like that, Em, but not to become famous. I guess I wanted to prove to myself I could do it. That I could accomplish something no one else had ever been able to. That I was more than hot air and empty promises." Jake laughed to himself.

"I even hoped that one day your father would be proud of his little brother. Now I've squandered most of his money, too."

"I haven't had a very successful career at finding treasure. It's been one failure after another," Jake admitted. "This was my last chance to make up for all those losses. I really thought we could get it. We had the right equipment, a good crew and the best technology. Damn, we were close!"

Jake wearily rubbed his temples.

"You two better get to bed. Doug's right. It'll be a long, hard day tomorrow and we'll need your help. Good night," he said, dismissing us.

"Good night," I said, getting up and starting back to the tents.

"'Night," Joel added.

We left Uncle Jake alone, staring into the fire's dying embers.

Ever since I was a little girl, I had admired Uncle Jake's optimism, his enthusiasm and energy, and his courage to try what most people only dreamed about. Sometimes I felt he was the heart of the Morgan family; a brilliant star around whom we all revolved. No matter what happened, you knew Uncle Jake would be there to laugh at whatever life threw at him. It hurt to hear him sound like he'd finally been beaten.

As Joel and I returned to our tents, we agreed it was time to return the favour. It was up to us to save Uncle Jake.

25

Descent into Darkness

OUR plan lost its lustre in the dark chill of that pre-dawn morning. Last night it seemed simple. I'd lower Joel into the pit with the hydraulic winch, he'd squeeze through the broken pipe at 40 metres, fill a bag full of treasure and come back out — instant heroes!

But now, looking into the blackness of the grave-like pit, it was like looking down an elevator shaft. This was a far cry from sneaking out to dig up the stone markers. The pit had become unstable, and there was the ongoing mystery of the rising water. Despite clogging the two underground flood tunnels and continued pumping, water was still getting in. And it was gaining on us, rising slowly with each passing minute.

The greatest danger was that the drainage pipe could collapse the rest of the way while Joel was inside of it. If that happened, I'd have no way to get him out.

I helped Joel into the seat harness by tightening the straps — the same straps used by mountain climbers and window washers. All Joel's weight would be on his hips so he could descend comfortably in a seated position. Joel nervously tied a bowline around the locking carabiner that hung from his waist harness, just as Jake had taught him. For good measure, I added half a dozen square knots with the loose end of the blue nylon line. We tugged at it to test it. One thing was for sure, the knots wouldn't slip.

"All set!" I said.

"Yeah," Joel said, his teeth chattering. "Me too! Hurry before I chicken out."

I couldn't tell if Joel was cold or scared, but I figured it was probably a little of both.

Joel took one of the helmets Doug had designed. It had a strong light attached to the front, like a coal miner, with a two-way radio. Joel positioned the receiver into his ear and adjusted the microphone suspended in front of his mouth. He snapped the chin strap. He was ready.

"Okay, I'm turning on the headset," I said, pushing the remote power button on the control panel.

"Testing, testing," Joel said into the microphone.

His voice boomed throughout the camp, rattling the speaker mounted near the hydraulic hoist.

"Too loud!" I thought, and lowered the volume. There was no way Jake or Doug would let us go through with this if either of them woke up. I nervously looked over to Jake's still and darkened tent. So far so good. I put on the other headset and plugged it into the terminal.

"Can you hear me?" I asked Joel.

"Loud and clear!" he said. "Let's go for it!"

"If I have any problems I'll call Jake," I said, trying to sound reassuring. Now I was starting to shiver.

Joel picked up the burlap bag and tucked it into his belt. "When I come back this will be full of doubloons!" he said with forced bravado.

"Good luck."

"Lower away!" were his last words before I carefully engaged the automatic hoist to start letting out line.

"Lowering away!" I called out.

The drum roller slowly turned, letting out line. Joel leaned backward over the hole in a sitting position, holding the line in front of him with one hand. And then he was gone.

"Okay, Joel, you're doing great!" I said into my microphone. "I'm going to speed it up just a bit."

"Okay," he replied tentatively.

I watched the green luminous display reflect his depth and adjusted the dials to speed up the drum until it was spinning faster than I realized.

"Three metres…six…nine," I read the control panel.

"Slow down, slow down!" Joel's voice boomed. "You're going to kill me!"

I did my best to slow the controls. It was harder than I expected.

"That's better," Joel said. "It's really dark down here and you'll bang me into the walls if you let me down too fast."

"Okay, sorry," I said. "I have to control both knobs at the same time and…"

"I know, Em," the voice over the speaker replied. "This is better. Keep it nice and slow like this."

"Eighteen point five, 19.2, 19.5, 19.8, 20.1," I called out

the depth from the console so Joel would know how far down he was and how much farther he had to go.

"It's really getting black," Joel said. "I can't see the bottom yet, but the pipe is getting narrower."

"Twenty-three, 23.4, 23.8, 24.2," I called out. "It's going to get even narrower. I better slow it down."

It was hard to adjust both controls at the same time. Seven months of physical therapy had helped a lot, but I hoped we weren't making a fatal mistake.

"Twenty-seven point four, 27.7, 28, 28.3," I reported.

"My ears are popping," Joel said. His voice was beginning to sound scratchy. "I think I see something reflecting down there, way below me. Can you slow it down more, Em?"

"I'm trying," I called back, but I couldn't adjust the controls any better to slow his descent.

"How deep am I now?"

"Thirty-five, 35.4, 35.8," I answered. His voice was full of static now and it was much harder to hear.

"It's the drainage pipe!" Joel called out. "I can see the jack that Jake put in yesterday. That's what's reflecting my headlamp. Em, slow up! I'm going to bang into it. Em, STOP!"

I stopped the rope drum an instant after Joel yelled. The brake was the easiest part to control. The one thing I had to remember was not to push the reverse lever while the drum was going in the other direction. Doug had warned that a sudden reversal in power could over-pressurize the system and possibly burst the hydraulic lines.

A low groaning, grating sound could be heard over the speaker.

"Joel, do you hear that? What's that sound?" I asked.

"It's the walls of the piping," he answered nervously. "The joints are making a weird noise, like metal scraping on metal. It's creepy!"

"Joel, I really don't like the sound of this. You want out?" I asked. There was a long silence.

"No. I'm okay," Joel finally answered.

"But it sounds terrible down there," I said.

"Em," Joel's scratchy voice echoed throughout the campsite. "I saw it! The lid of the chest; a minute ago, but the water's covered it up. I can make it, Em. I can do it! I can fit through the pipe. I can reach the treasure!"

I was beginning to have real doubts about this. It was now or never.

"All right," I said with finality. "Let's do this fast as possible. Get through and take whatever you can, 'cause after that I'm pulling you out!"

"I'll have to go headfirst so I can grab something," Joel explained. "Once I'm in the pipe, I can't turn around."

"Upside down through that narrow pipe? Be careful, Joel," I said with more emotion in my voice than I expected.

Forty metres below, Joel awkwardly spun himself around so he was hanging upside down from the rope harness. On the surface, I could hear only laboured breathing and groaning pipes.

"Ready," he said.

"I'll start lowering you now," I said, trying to sound reassuring. "Nice and easy. The chest should be about six metres lower."

I gently worked the controls so that the hoist drum began inching out more line.

"I'm through!" Joel's voice announced triumphantly over the speaker. "But it looks like the water's getting deeper."

The metal drum continued to turn, gradually lowering Joel deeper and deeper through the last narrow length of drainpipe. I could hear the sound of my own heart pounding.

Joel had wriggled through a long, empty drainpipe back home on a dare, and in swimming class he could dive deeper than any of his friends, but the thought of him doing both at the same time made my stomach churn with fear.

"I'm almost to the water," Joel said. It was getting hard to understand him through the static. "But I'm going to get pretty wet going down to the chest."

"How deep is it?" I asked nervously.

"I'm not sure. I think about two metres or so," he answered. His words were breaking up.

"This isn't what we planned," I said. "I'll give you 30 seconds, then I'm pulling you out. Hold your breath and go for it!"

It sounded like Joel answered, "Okay, here I go," but the static was so bad I couldn't be sure. He was breathing very hard. Then I remembered something.

"Joel, the headset will short out..." but before I could finish, the static ceased. The microphone and headlamp weren't waterproof.

I wasn't sure how long Joel could hold his breath, but I knew it was at least 30 seconds. As I started the timer, I could see the light come on in Uncle Jake's tent from the corner of my eye.

Plunging headfirst into the frigid salt water, Joel would have been engulfed in total blackness. He was completely cut off from the surface. I only hoped he was prepared for the disorienting effect of the cold, black water. I felt claustrophobic, thinking of him bravely trying to wriggle through the narrow flooded pipe.

"Come on, Joel, you can do it," I said to myself. "Just hold on a little longer."

When Jake reached me at the console 20 seconds had clicked away on the timer. It took him only a moment to assess the entire situation. He was horrified.

"What do you think you're doing?" he shouted angrily.

Doug ran to where Jake stood.

"What's going on?" Doug asked innocently.

"Is Joel down there?" Uncle Jake said pointing to the pit, glaring at me as he waited for an answer.

"Yes." I couldn't look Jake in the eyes. I suddenly felt stupid and foolish.

"Doug, take over and pull him back to the surface!" Jake said with authority.

Doug quickly slid in beside me, smoothly assuming control without interrupting the slowly turning metal drum.

"We were just trying to help you," I said weakly.

"Em, I appreciate that, I truly do. But you don't understand how dangerous it is," Jake said.

"Damn!" Doug swore. "She's lowered him all the way to the bottom!"

"What!" Jake gasped.

"But it's okay," I tried to explain. "I gave him 30 seconds to grab some treasure from the chest. I just started pulling him out. The water is only two metres deep."

"It's seven metres deep and rising — fast! The lower pipe is completely flooded!" Doug said with alarm, having turned on the water sensors I had forgotten. "The water is gushing in Jake! He's still underwater!"

The timer on the console read 45 seconds.

"Faster!" Jake snapped. "Get him out of there!"

For the first time in my life I sensed real fear in my uncle's voice. Then the metal drum that was taking in the line suddenly froze.

"It's stopped!" I called out.

"It's jammed at 40 metres," Doug yelled.

Jake knew immediately what the problem was.

"We're crushing him against the jack!" Jake yelled. "If he blacks out we'll never get him out!"

What little air Joel had must have escaped as the harness wrenched him sideways against the narrow opening of the crushed pipe. The timer read 58 seconds. The water was still rising. Joel was unable to move and desperate for oxygen. There seemed to be no way out.

26

Rescued!

JAKE lunged toward the delicate gearing and without thinking did the one thing he had repeatedly warned against. He slammed it into reverse while it was still trying to pull forward. The sudden reversal in the hoist's hydraulic torque was too much for the frail system. It slammed to a stop. The thin hydraulic lines running along the inside of the hoist's protective cowling burst, spraying a deadly shower of scalding fluid in front of the delicate controls.

Doug leaped to the hoist. He bravely reached through the burning liquid, attempting to reach the awkwardly positioned controls at the back of the long casing.

"Turn it to manual!" Jake shouted. "We're drowning him!"

But the searing pain was too much. Doug couldn't ignore the burning long enough to reset the small dials. Twice he tried, each time withdrawing his arm bearing terrible burn marks.

"I can't reach it!" he said, terror in his normally calm voice.

The timer read 1:15.

I reached the hoist before Jake and pushed Doug aside. Joel was drowning. We all knew it. Jake and Doug needed someone who could reach through the scalding liquid and reset the dials to manual. They needed someone whose arm could stand the pain. They needed me.

As I reached through the burning fluid I knew I was the only one who could save Joel. Everything seemed to fall into place. Here was my purpose. Here was the answer to all my agonizing questions of "why me?" To save Joel. Behind me, Jake's instructions sounded distant and far away, "Both dials need to be reset to zero..." I painlessly adjusted the dials as the hydraulic fluid melted portions of my prosthetic arm.

The timer's green display now read 1:30.

We had to give Joel enough time to climb, upside down, back through the narrow portion of the crushed pipe. But how much longer could he hold out? We watched the seconds pass until the timer flashed 1:40. It was the longest 10 seconds of my life.

"Go!" Jake yelled.

Jake and Doug were at opposite sides of the large metal drum around which the blue line was wound. On Jake's command they began turning the hoist by hand with the metal handles they'd inserted into its sides.

"It's still moving. He must be through!" Jake triumphantly exclaimed. "Faster!"

Faster and faster they cranked the spinning drum, racing against time to save Joel from the flooding pit.

"Twenty-nine, 28.6, 28.2, 28, 27," I called off the depth

readings as Jake and Doug madly spun the metal cylinder, bringing Joel closer and closer to the surface. "Twenty, 18.2, 17.4, 16.6," I breathlessly continued.

"Faster!" Jake shouted, but I doubted it was humanly possible to spin the drum any faster.

"Nine...six...three. He's up!" I shouted.

Jake and Doug quickly pulled Joel to one side of the hole where he collapsed on the ground, gasping for air. He coughed violently for several minutes as he replenished his oxygen-starved body. He was weak and slightly incoherent, but safe. It was the first time in years I'd hugged him like that. He was alive and that's all that mattered. I was half-crying and half-laughing. I felt Uncle Jake's arms encircling both of us. He had tears in the corner of his eyes. Doug stood back, uncomfortable with all the emotion, but with a wide grin across his face.

Jake and I helped Joel out of the harness. He was shivering from cold and exhaustion. Doug draped a blanket over his shoulders. His face was a patchwork of bruises and scrapes — the worst of which were bleeding. His left hand was covered in blood.

"You've got guts kid," Doug said, cradling his own burned arm. "No one else I know could have done that!"

"Thanks," Joel replied weakly. The colour was beginning to return to his face.

"Let's get you into the tent and patched up," Jake said to Joel. "You're pretty scraped up. Probably didn't do you much good when the winch tried to pull you through the collapsed opening."

"I felt like an egg being pulled through a keyhole!" Joel laughed tiredly.

"You can fill us in on what happened," Jake said. "I'll look at those burns on your arm after that, Doug."

"Better get him first," Doug smiled. "He's the hero!"

Doug and I sat on the canvas cot while Jake attended to Joel's injuries. Joel slumped in a folding chair while Jake applied ointment and bandages to his face.

"Do you feel up to telling us what happened down there?" Jake asked.

"I guess so," Joel quietly replied. "Once I hit the water my headlamp went out. I'd never been in such cold water. It was like being stabbed in the face with needles. And it was completely black. I couldn't see anything. I could feel the dirt and muck in the water around me. The water was really more like thin mud. I guess I was pretty scared," Joel said sheepishly.

"Hey," Doug said, looking Joel in the eyes, "only a fool wouldn't have been scared down there. Bravery doesn't mean you're never afraid; it's about doing something even when you're afraid of it."

"I dove down, kicking to get deeper," Joel continued. "Then I felt the top of the treasure chest, but I couldn't see anything. I felt around and found a hole in the top of it."

"That would have been our auger drill hole," Jake said.

"Well, it wasn't big enough to get my hand through, so I started ripping at the sides of the hole and pieces of the lid began to break away."

"Dry rot," Jake said. "What happened then?"

"I let go for an instant and started floating back up away from the chest. So I kicked as hard as I could, and reached out to grab whatever was in the chest."

"It's amazing that you did all that without being able to see anything," I said.

"I reached out with both hands. I could feel the sides of the chest between my arms, but I couldn't tell which hand was inside and which was outside. I grabbed as hard as I could. Something jagged cut my left hand," Joel said, extending his blood-covered hand for us to see, "but my right hand found a mound of gold doubloons! I had a whole handful of treasure!

"I sort of cradled the coins against my chest, like this," Joel said, demonstrating. "That's when I felt you guys start to pull me out. I was still upside down in the drainpipe, but I realized something was wrong. I could feel myself being raised, but there wasn't any air. I wasn't sure how much longer I could hold my breath."

"The entire lower section was flooded," Doug said.

"Then I could feel you pull much faster. That's when I smashed into something. I guess it was the jack you put in yesterday. The little bit of air I still had escaped. The harness just kept pulling and pulling. I was squished so tightly against the jack I couldn't get out. I remember hearing my heart pounding like a drum inside my ears. I really thought I was going to drown," Joel said.

"You would have if it wasn't for Em," Jake said. "She saved your life, Joel. If she hadn't reset the winch, we couldn't have gotten you out."

Joel looked at me in a way I'll never forget.

"Thanks, Em," he said. It didn't sound like much, but I knew he meant it with all his heart.

"Everything was spinning around," Joel continued, "my ears were ringing, and I felt like my lungs were going to explode. Then the rope went slack. I had room to squeeze back out through the crushed part of the pipe.

"I had to get through upside down, but I couldn't do it with just one hand. I honestly tried as hard as I could, Uncle Jake. I really did."

Joel's voice had a tremor to it, and I could tell he was fighting back tears. In his exhausted state, the feeling that he'd let down Uncle Jake was almost too much for him.

"I know you did, Joel. It's all right, it really is," Jake said. "Go ahead with your story."

"I needed both hands to get out," Joel said. "I opened my right hand to grab onto the pipe and lost all the treasure. I could feel some of it as it headed back down to the bottom of the pit.

"I got through the pipe, but I was so dizzy, I couldn't tell which way was up. I think I was about to pass out. The harness jerked me up to the air just in time."

Jake, Doug and I were silent for a moment after Joel had finished. We were all a little frightened at how close Joel had come to drowning.

"I'm sorry I had to drop them," Joel apologized.

"It doesn't matter," Jake said. "You're safe and that's more important than a handful of coins."

"But it would have solved the mystery for you!" Joel

said, looking into Jake's eyes.

"I suppose it would have," Jake said thoughtfully. "But when we came so close, and still came away empty-handed, it makes you wonder if it's somehow meant to remain a mystery."

"Well it won't be solved anytime soon," Doug said. He had rechecked the control sensors before we came into the tent. "The lower length of drain pipe completely collapsed — flat as a pancake! And the water was still rising. There must be a third flood tunnel somewhere down there. All our work and the whole thing's coming apart at the seams."

Doug had been looking at Joel when suddenly his eyes widened.

"Joel," he asked, "what position were you in when you dropped the treasure? Upside down?"

Jake and I looked at Doug, wondering what he was getting at.

"Yes, well, no," Joel said, trying to remember. "I was sort of scrunched sideways, trying to get through the smashed pipe."

Doug reached out and snatched something off the front of Joel's wet shirt.

"I asked because I think one of your gold coins got stuck on your shirt pocket."

"What?" Joel exclaimed.

All eyes were riveted on Doug's hand as he slowly opened it. It was a J-shaped piece of brown metal.

"Sorry," Doug said. "It's a badly corroded link of chain — very, very old, but still just a piece of chain. The broken edge must have caught on your shirt when you dropped them."

Joel was crestfallen. Jake put a comforting hand on Joel's shoulder.

"You must have grabbed a handful of chain — it's probably what once bound the chest closed," he said to Joel.

"We must have cut it with the drill," Doug observed.

"It sure felt like gold," Joel said, picking up the corroded link to examine it.

"But it was pitch-black after your light went out," I said, feeling a little sorry for him.

"It's not your fault."

"She's right, Joel," Doug added. "Any of us would have thought the same thing."

"Can I keep it?" Joel asked.

"You've certainly earned it," Jake smiled. "Now let's have a look at the hand you cut. From the look of how much you've bled, it probably needs stitches."

Joel put his left hand on the table in front of him so Jake could clean and dress the wound. His palm was caked with drying blood and mud.

"This will hurt a bit," Jake told him, "but I've got to wash it off and clean out the wound."

Jake squirted disinfectant onto the palm to wash away the blood and dirt. Joel winced as the liquid found its way into the open wound. After a few moments, Jake had a clear view. Jake paled as he looked down at Joel's palm.

"What is it?" Joel asked, straining to see what concerned Jake so much. "How bad is it?"

"Doug," Jake said in an odd voice, "you'd better have a look at this."

Now I was afraid. I had gory images of his hand hanging by a thread, or cut down to the bone. Doug leaned over Joel's hand.

"Incredible!" he gasped.

"What is it? Let me see!" Joel insisted. "What's wrong?"

Jake and Doug moved away from the table so Joel could see. I leaned over to look. Deeply imbedded in the palm of Joel's left hand were two large black thorns.

27

Wealth of Ages

THE two thorns were tested separately. The largest was sent
to the Radiocarbon Dating Lab in Ottawa, and the second to
the Canadian Centre for Accelerator Mass Spectrometry in
Toronto. The results were disappointedly the same —
inconclusive. For some unexplainable reason, the thorns did
not respond to analysis as expected. The technicians were at
a complete loss to explain why.

The pit itself partially collapsed after Joel escaped.
Onrushing water put pressure on the aluminum extension
piping, splitting open nearly every seam. Silt-filled sludge
oozed back into the pit, starting the natural refilling process.
In time, this gradual healing would leave nothing more than
another small scar on Oak Island.

As for my uncle, the mystery surrounding the second
chest made Jake an instant celebrity — magazine covers,
radio talk shows, public television specials and, of course,
offers from several historians to head up their treasure-
hunting ventures.

Yet true to his word on that star-filled night, it wasn't
about the money. Rather than sell the thorns to speculative

collectors, Jake convinced his financial backers to donate them to the Museum of History. He said it was the easiest sale he had ever made.

Joel never expected to receive so much attention for the courage he displayed that morning when he willingly descended into the pit. But as the newspapers liked to point out, those two thorns may have drawn the blood of two people, and one of them was my little brother.

But were the thorns genuine, or another ancient hoax; and what else lies buried in the second treasure chest? Perhaps no one will ever know. I often wonder if something really does guard the island's long-kept secret.

As for me, something had died inside of me when the accident took my arm, something inside I never thought I'd have again — hope. I guess that's the treasure I found on Oak Island that summer — a reason for hope. And for that, I felt the most blessed of all.

AGMV Marquis

MEMBER OF SCABRINI MEDIA

Quebec, Canada
2002